TAMED BY THE OUTLAW

A WHAT HAPPENS IN  STORY

MICHELLE SHARP

Entangled Publishing, LLC
2614 South Timberline Road
Suite 109
Fort Collins, CO 80525
Visit our website at www.entangledpublishing.com.

Lovestruck is an imprint of Entangled Publishing, LLC.

Edited by Lisa Bone
Cover design by Heather Howland
Cover art from iStock

Manufactured in the United States of America

First Edition August 2015

To my very best friend, Cindy Nieukirk. Thank you for the million ways you support me. The list is endless and grows with each passing year. Love you bunches—Michelle

Chapter One

Apparently, when social media catches you making a fool of yourself, people crawl out of the woodwork to see what a spectacular dumbass you are in person. Romance author Jessica Jameson closed the convention room door, turning away. She hoped a long, deep breath would ease the urge to puke. "Holy crap. I am *not* this interesting."

Jessie's agent, Lila Kent, reopened the heavy wooden door and looked into the Grand Ballroom of Las Vegas's Masquerade Hotel for herself. "Wow. There *are* a lot of people here. A local reporter and TV camera too. That's unusual for a romance conference. Good thing they switched our session to the ballroom."

"No. *No*, it's *not* a good thing. You said a room with a handful of people in it. Where I could casually chat with fans and other authors. That"—she pointed to the ballroom—"is a lynch mob. You said I didn't have to prepare anything. What the hell am I supposed to talk about for an hour?"

"You're kidding, right?" The Bronx accent spilled out of her agent's little body with a badass New York brashness that people instinctively knew better than to screw with.

Jessie certainly knew better. Lila had been kicking ass in the publishing world longer than Jessie had been alive.

Lila folded her arms across her chest. "You're Jessie James. *Outlaw* of the romance world. You've got a smoking hot book sitting at number one on the New York Times best-seller list. *That's* what you're supposed to talk about."

Lila reached up and put her hands on Jessie's shoulders. She was the size of a pixie—couldn't reach five-foot-nothing with heels on. "And let's be honest, the amount of crazy in your life could fill a three-day workshop. This is just a one-hour question and answer session. Easy breezy."

Jessie begged to differ. There were twenty times more people here than any other Q&A she'd been a part of. And she knew some of them were going to ask about more than her books.

Lila must have recognized her look of nausea and took pity. "Lauren and I will be on the panel with you. Just be yourself and answer the questions." Her tone was much gentler this time. "You've done this before. Fans can't get enough of you. But watch your mouth. Your cursing gets out of hand when you're nervous."

Jessie scrubbed her hands over her face.

"Stop it." Lila smacked at her hands. "You're messing up your makeup. Why are you freaking about this?"

Jessie loved chatting with fans, but usually she was on a panel with other authors and could deflect any questions that made her uncomfortable. Not the case today. She had only her agent and editor to save her ass. "It's just that there are so many people this time." Sweat trickled through her hairline. "I'm hot. Are you hot? Why is it so hot in here?"

"Because you're wearing black leather from head to toe and it's like six hundred degrees outside." Lila looked her up and down. "At least take off the jacket."

Jessie slid her favorite jacket from her shoulders, exposing a black, silky tank with LOVE ROCKS scrolled in sequins across her breasts.

"On second thought, put the jacket back on and suffer." Her agent's Bronx accent made the last word sound like *suffa*.

It made Jessie snicker. "What? It's a romance conference. Everyone wears sequins in Vegas. It's funny. Besides, you're the one that wanted to brand me as the bad girl."

"Yet you're worried about being boring?"

Jessie smiled and stepped farther away from the dreaded door. Lila was right. She could do this. She'd worked a long time for this kind of success. For years, she'd kept a second job to pay the bills. Now that her romance series had exploded, she could afford to focus solely on the one thing she loved most—writing.

This is a good thing.

She paced back and forth a few times, frankly a little stunned that this many people were gathered to hear her speak. Hell, a couple of years ago no one gave a damn who she was. She wasn't any different now than she'd ever been, except she'd sold a few more books.

Slipping back into her jacket, she yanked her hair out from under her collar. As it fell back around her face, she looked up, straight into the eyes of Grayson Reynolds—CEO of Reynolds & Reynolds Publishing, sex god, and asshat extraordinaire.

Standing just a few tiny inches from Mr. Large-and-in-charge made an uncomfortable heat radiate from her face again. "What the hell are you doing here?"

Asshat lifted an amused brow, but his gaze never faltered from her chest. "Interesting choice of shirts."

She tugged her jacket closed.

Lila lunged between them like an Olympic long jumper. "Mr. Reynolds. I…uh… I apologize. Jessie doesn't visit the corporate offices much. She obviously has you confused with someone else."

Nope.

Jessie knew exactly who the Ivy League prick was, despite the fact he'd given her a false name to get her into bed a year ago.

When she'd slept with him, she had no idea he was *the* Reynolds heir, in line to be CEO of her publishing house. Absolutely no idea he'd be the one signing her paychecks. And she certainly hadn't known he was a cold-blooded snake, cruel enough to make love to a woman and then sneak out as if he were a thief in the night.

But she sure as hell knew it now.

"I know who he is." Jessie zipped her jacket, taking care to cover her LOVE ROCKS. Especially since asshat's sultry stare had her body responding much like it did the first time she'd laid eyes on him.

"Your editor is not going to make it to the conference. She was on the way to the airport this morning and started having contractions. She headed to the hospital, and I got on the plane in her place."

Jessie's heart raced even faster. Lauren was a kick-ass

editor, but she'd also become a good friend. "Is she going to be okay? There's nothing wrong with the baby is there?"

"I just talked to her husband again. Sounds like they're both fine, but the doctors want her off her feet," he said.

"Thank God." Jessie felt relief buzz all the way down to her toes. Lauren and her husband had been trying to have children for years. "Good. I'll call her when my session is over." And okay, she was moderately grateful that tall, dark, and heartless was courteous enough to deliver the news before her session started. Both she and Lila had already discussed their concerns that Lauren hadn't showed yet.

In the interest of time—and because of a death glare from Lila—Jessie refrained from any further derogatory remarks.

She decided to throw out a little false bravado and pray Grayson Alexander Reynolds *the third* crawled back under whatever rock he'd slithered from. "Thank you for informing us."

The moderator of the session poked his head out of the door. "Ms. James, are you ready? I'll be introducing you in just a few minutes."

"Sure. We'll be there." Lila answered for her. "But we're down a person. Lauren Evans is ill and won't be on the panel today. You might want to mention that to the crowd. The program states that an editor from R and R will be answering questions with Jessie."

Lila rocked and was already doing damage control. With Lauren out, Jessie was confident her agent would jump in and do her best to field some of the questions inside the ballroom. Now, if Lila could chase Grayson away, Jessie vowed to give her the biggest Christmas bonus ever.

Instead, Ivy League turned to the moderator. "I'll be taking Lauren's place on the panel today. I'm Grayson Reynolds, CEO of Reynolds and Reynolds. I'll be happy to answer any questions from a publisher's perspective."

In Jessie's head, the words echoed like she'd been dropped into a bottomless canyon. Finally, she managed a weak, "What?"

Which didn't come close to fully expressing what she really meant.

What the fuck?

Or, *Not in this lifetime.*

Or, *I'll sit on a panel with you when wild monkeys fly out of my ass.*

Grayson turned to Jessie. "I'm taking Lauren's place today."

"*No.* I mean…why would you do that?" She looked desperately at Lila for backup. "We certainly don't need you in there."

"I beg to differ. R and R is my company. In spite of your popularity, you tend to be a bit…"

He paused, and *oh man*, she just knew he was mentally running down a checklist of insults he was refraining from verbalizing.

"Unconventional," he finally said. "You are one of my authors. And I'm responsible."

"You? Responsible?" To her mind, Grayson Reynolds was about as responsible as using a condom made of fishnet. Her eye twitched from the effort of restraining the comment.

"You're not afraid to sit next to me, are you, *outlaw*?" His voice turned low and condescending. He emphasized her nickname like it was the filthiest word that had ever passed his lips.

Which was ironic, since she knew, intimately, the scandalous things that poured out of the man's mouth in the heat of the moment. "Yes. Afraid I might catch something."

"Don't worry. I don't bite."

"Tell it to the scar on my shoulder." Jessie narrowed her gaze. "That's sure as hell not how I remember it."

Lila shrieked and gave Jessie a bony little elbow to the ribs as she lunged to intercept the rapid-fire insults winging back and forth. But before they could be pushed to neutral corners, asshat held up one dangerous finger.

Then he unleashed a cold, withering stare on Lila. "I'm going to need a moment with your author."

Don't you dare make me talk to him alone!

Jessie did her best to transfer the mental demand to Lila through pleading eyes and her own version of a Jedi mind trick. But clearly the Force was not with Jessie, because Lila turned and abandoned ship into the ballroom. *No Christmas bonus for you*, Jessie decided as the door clicked shut.

And she was left.

Alone.

With the bastard that had delivered more orgasms in one night than all the other men in her life combined.

Then had disappeared like he'd been as make-believe as a hero in one of her romance novels.

Fine. Maybe now was the time to set some boundaries. They'd ignored each other for a year. Enough was enough. She glared at Grayson. "I have no idea what you're trying to pull. But when I discovered, quite by accident, that you were the new CEO of R and R, I bent over backwards to fulfill my contract and stay far, *far* out of your way. I have never come to your office and made trouble. Do you really need to come here and mess with me?"

"It's a romance conference. I own a publishing house. You write for my company. It's not rocket science. Did you honestly think we'd never cross paths again?" He arrogantly held up his hands as if to shush her before she spoke again. "Besides. I think it's time we clear the air. In spite of what happened a year ago, we both need to move on. I may not have been completely honest about who I was, but in all fairness, you didn't give me a chance to explain."

"I didn't give you a chance to explain?" Jessie let out a sarcastic laugh and poked him—hard—in the chest. "Here's a piece of advice for you, Ivy League. Lies tend to piss women off. Find the time to explain who you are *before* you put your mouth on a woman's breast."

Grayson watched Jessie's superb ass stalk furiously away. Today, she was all black leather, sequins, and soft, full, red-painted lips.

She made him think of sex. She made him think of the sex he'd had with her.

Perfect.

Why did he go there every single time he saw her? Probably because in spite of his wounded pride, he wasn't blind. Nor did he have memory loss. He knew exactly what those lips were capable of.

It was just too goddamned bad she was the devil.

He looked up and saw a giant poster for her new book. The quote on the front read: *Erotic Suspense with Heart.*

Ha. Erotic he had no problem believing. Suspense, maybe so. But last year she'd fucked him into a sexual coma, and as far as he knew, hadn't looked back since. So the heart part...not so much.

Which begged the question: why the hell had she jumped down his throat?

Because women are complete enigmas. One of his grandpa's favorite mottos.

It occurred to him that he had not given gramps full genius props for that little gem of wisdom. Not until he'd sparred with Jessie James.

Didn't matter. He just wanted to be rid of her. He wanted to be rid of her books in his company. He wanted to be rid of her face plastered on every piece of advertising material that passed across his desk. In fact, he wanted to be rid of the company's entire romance line.

If he could pull off a weekend of being civil to Jessica Jameson, he'd be rid of her, the frivolous romance division she wrote for, and, finally, the mind-fuck of being naked with the outlaw herself.

And as much as he loved and respected his grandfather, R&R needed a facelift. The romance division had a few authors putting up big numbers. Like Jessie. But overall, sales were soft. And as far as respect, to his mind it was lacking there, too. He wanted the big names. Patterson. King. Clancy. Pulitzer Prize winners. He doubted very seriously that was going to happen pushing sex and love with the same hokey happily-ever-after in every book.

Five months ago his grandfather had suffered a mild heart attack, and Grayson had stepped in as the new CEO of Reynolds & Reynolds publishing. R&R wasn't just a business or publishing house. R&R was pride and years of dedication, built from decades of his grandfather's grueling work.

Now his grandfather had left him a legacy, and he intended to run that legacy until R&R was one of the most respected publishing houses in the world.

R&R needed changes. The first big one was going to be dropping the romance division like a bad habit. Last week, King of Hearts Publishing had offered to buy R&R's romance line for a cool twenty million dollars—provided that Jessie James and her wildly successful romance series came with the deal.

A sign from God himself.

The fly in the ointment was that selling the romance division of R&R voided Jessie's contract. Legally, she'd have the right to publish the rest of her series anywhere she liked. Which meant he sure as hell didn't want to approach Lila Kent with the deal first. The little gremlin had nothing but dollar signs in her eyes. Jessie James may have been a wild card, but if he could get her onboard with the King of Hearts contract, Lila would be easier to maneuver.

He looked at his watch, trying to decide if he had time for a whisky or two—or ten—before he had to walk into the ballroom. But he knew the answer before he'd ever glanced at the time.

He made the decision to get on the plane this morning for a very specific reason. And that reason just stomped away like she'd prefer a lobotomy over sitting next to him for the next hour. Too bad. By the end of the weekend, he planned to convince Jessie James to sign with King of Hearts. Surely they could be civil long enough to have a real conversation about a move that would be mutually beneficial for both of them. Although her go-to-hell attitude didn't look promising.

But he was a Reynolds. And when a Reynolds had a goal, the goal got achieved. If he had to suck it up and deal with Jessie for a weekend, so be it. If she wanted an apology, he'd grovel just to be rid of her. If he had to play the poor, sorry schmuck, okay.

Hell, if she wanted her ass kissed—fine.

Actually, he'd kissed her ass before and it was, in fact, a world-class ass. As was the rest of her. Tall and curvy. Long, lean legs. And dark hair that waved around her head with wild attitude. Which was nothing but prophetic when you thought about it—even her hair was probably a bitch to tame.

Unfortunately—he knew from experience—so was the outlaw!

Chapter Two

Jessie walked into the ballroom and made her way toward the front. One good thing about seeing Grayson—anger had overtaken her nerves. There were three chairs at the long table up on the stage. She dropped into the middle one.

Lila was already seated. She glared at Jessie with a red face and her mouth etched into a thin line, looking like she wanted to explode. The microphones weren't on yet. Still, Lila scooted discretely back from the table. "What the hell was that all about?"

"Nothing. It's fine."

Lila glared. Not the usual scary one, but the rare terrifying one she only unleashed in extreme situations. "You betta be straight with me, ace. And I sure as hell betta not lose a huge contract because you two bumped uglies and he's pissed off about it."

The room was staggeringly loud, and the moderator had stepped away from the stage. Jessie desperately wanted to melt into a puddle on the floor, but she decided Lila would do less physical harm with three or four hundred witnesses. Now seemed like the safest time to fess up. She turned her head and whispered close to Lila's ear. "I met him a year ago at this same conference. We sat next to each other in the bar, we had a few drinks, talked for hours. I thought he seemed like a great guy."

In spite of her reckless image that had been grossly exaggerated in public, Jessie considered herself almost boring. Never in her life had she participated in a one-night stand—until Grayson. Now she understood why they were, in general, an epically bad idea. "He lied about his name. Told me he was Grayson Smith and that he worked in advertising."

"And," Lila said.

Jessie blinked. Her throat burned with shame and stupidity. "And yes, I slept with him. But he snuck out before I woke. So that's it. He lied, used me, then snuck away. A real class act."

Lila's mouth dropped open, snapped shut, then dropped open again. "Don't you think it would have been wise to mention this to me before now?"

"Yes. Probably. But I didn't know who he was until the headline broke that he'd been made the new CEO of R and R. What could I do but write my books and stay as far away from the R and R offices as possible?"

Jessie shrugged it off, trying to downplay the disastrous mistake. "I'm sorry I lost it. I was just shocked to see him here, but I'm over it."

Lila leaned back in her chair and narrowed her eyes. "Well, you betta get over it, and in a big hurry."

"Hey, he was the one that used me—"

Lila held up her hand. "You made a choice to bang a guy you didn't know at a professional conference. I don't know the particulars. I don't *want* to know. But right now, you and I are both riding a one-in-a-million wave of success in this industry. R and R is the reason for it. So when he walks in here, you're going to smile, play nice, and pray to the god of publishing we're both not out on our asses."

Jessie looked up. "Great. Here he comes." She glanced at Lila and could tell her agent had reined in her temper and shifted into damage control guru.

"Let me tell you somethin' kid," Lila whispered. "All these people are here to see you. Even if we're screwed with R and R, it's only one publishing company. Grayson Reynolds and R and R may be a thing of the past once your current contract is fulfilled, but these people will be fans forever."

Wow, Jessie thought. That was really profound and heartfelt for her brash little New York agent.

"So smile and don't be a bitch," Lila added.

Jessie did smile. As usual, Lila's advice was one part pat-on-the-back, mixed with two parts harsh-twist-of-the-arm. It was also spot-on.

She'd take the higher road. Be kind. Be friendly. Even to asshat. That's what the crowd would take away. Just a simple, uneventful Q&A. That was the best she could hope for.

She watched Grayson step up on stage.

He wore the CEO arrogance well. King of the universe in his navy suit and tie. Tall. Lean. Handsome. No one would guess that under all the mild mannered corporate layers lay a fiercely ripped body with a sexy tattoo and a seriously gifted penis.

She certainly hadn't expected it. Nor had she expected to

be so entranced by his harmless gray eyes, which darkened to coal as he watched a woman come.

The flashback struck like lightning. She shifted uncomfortably in her chair. Thank God no one could read her thoughts.

Lila kicked her shin. "Focus. On the crowd."

I am so screwed…

Grayson moved behind her and sat in the only vacant chair. His elbow and leg rested just inches from her own. An hour ago, she'd have bet the royalties from her new book that she would never have been sitting this close to Grayson Reynolds.

The moderator introduced the title of the session: "Ask the Outlaw Anything, featuring erotic romance writer Jessie James." He pointed to the two microphones in the room and explained that anyone who had a question should get in line.

About fifteen minutes in, Jessie had to admit things were going better than she expected. The crowd was huge and loud and fun. With the amount of choices people had in entertainment these days, it touched her that so many people had gathered to see her.

The typical questions came.

How does it feel to be number one on the New York Times *bestseller list?*

What are you writing after the Riding in the Night series is complete?

Lila and Grayson had both been mostly silent, letting her interact and joke with the audience. Despite Grayson's presence, she was having a great time. The crowd had grown excited and just a little bit rowdy. Some of the questions were shockingly personal, but she let loose and tried to have fun with it.

The next fan at the microphone asked, "Is there a special guy in your life who inspires your heroes to be such bad boys at times? Or are they completely made up?"

In her peripheral vision, Jessie saw Grayson's head turn toward her. "I'd say they're a combination of many experiences. Some of them mine. Others just stories I've heard from friends. I wanted the heroes to be heroic when it counts, but still believable. Let's face it, most men are jerks at some point, right? So they wouldn't be real unless they did a few boneheaded things."

The crowd, mostly female, erupted in laughter and agreed.

The same fan continued, "My book club just wanted to say we love your characters and hope you continue writing the Riders of the Night series. We've even forgiven Ian for lying about his identity and sneaking out on Tessa after they made love."

Lila made a noise in her throat like the warning growl of a rabid dog.

Jessie swallowed, ignored Lila, and risked a looked at Grayson, who looked puzzled but not particularly angry, which told her exactly what she wanted to know.

He hadn't read her last book.

If he had, he'd have recognized the subtle nuances of their lovemaking. Not to mention the obvious jab at his character for sneaking out the next morning. Probably not the smartest move she'd ever made, but she'd still been so pissed off when she'd written that scene.

The next lady at the mic giggled before she spoke. "Okay, my husband is here with me, and he bet me diamond earrings that I wouldn't really ask this question, so I'm going to ask it."

Jessie laughed and rubbed her hands together. "Boy, I bet this is a good one. Where is this husband of yours?"

The lady pointed, and a very embarrassed looking guy waved.

Jessie leaned close to the microphone. "Sir, did you promise your wife diamonds if she asks me a question?"

He nodded.

She had no idea why she'd been so nervous earlier because this was the crap she loved—joking and laughing with an audience. "Dude," Jessie teased. "You are sooo screwed."

The audience roared.

"Okay girlfriend, shoot. You've got several hundred witnesses if he tries to back out. I want to see a picture of these earrings. I'm thinking at least one carat."

Completely red-faced, the woman laughed and said, "I told my husband he needed to perform more like Ian did in the bedroom, but he says it's physically impossible for a man to have back to back orgasms with almost no recovery time, like Ian did. We just wondered if you researched that."

The crowd went wild laughing. The doors had opened and it was standing room only. The noise was insane and loud. Apparently, since she wrote erotica, people mistook her for some kind of sex expert. "Well, I'm not a doctor, and I've never even played one on TV, but I will say that I do know there are men capable of it." In fact, there was one sitting right next to her. But she'd gladly endure a public hanging before she'd risk even a glance at him. "And no, I will not divulge my resources on this particular research."

The crowd was still roaring when she noticed Grayson reach for one of her books and start to finger through it.

*H*oly *shit.* Grayson had been to rock concerts where there was less hooting and hollering going on. And worse, he was beginning to think he was the butt of a joke.

Inside a best-selling book.

That his company published.

Jessie James was a one-woman show, teasing and laughing with the audience. Being on this damn stage seemed as natural as breathing for her. And the shit people were asking. It was like being trapped on some hybrid of *Sex in the City* meets *Dr. Phil.*

What the fuck?

As CEO of a publishing house, he couldn't possibly read every book that passed through the doors. And he never read the romances. He trusted his staff. But he was sure going to read Jessie's. Like right now.

Why would his editors let her print something so personal? Okay. That was stupid. Obviously they didn't *know* the details had been personal, but he suspected they sure as shit had been.

"Over here. Go ahead." Jessie pointed to a lady in the audience.

"Do you get to pick the covers for your books? How close do the guys on the front look like what you've pictured in your head?"

Jessie laughed. "Well, I get some input. I describe my heroes, what I think they look like. But ultimately, the designers do their thing. And usually they do a pretty darn good job. I've had no complaints so far."

"Because the guy on the front of the Ian book is smoking hot," the lady at the mic said. "Do you know if that cover model is at this conference?"

"It just so happens that I know him well. His name is Stan Marcus, and I think he'll be wandering around the book signing tonight if you want a picture with him."

Grayson flipped the book shut, looked at the cover. The guy did kind of bear an eerie similarity to his own appearance. Same hair color, similar eyes, but the dude was huge and ripped. Grayson worked out, but this guy had to be on steroids or something. And fake Fabio didn't likely run a multimillion dollar publishing business. The bonehead obviously had nothing better to do than lift weights for a living.

"Can you tell us about the charity you're involved with? The one that received over half a million dollars after your appearance on Celebrity Challenge?"

Grayson looked up. Finally, a real question. It was a local news reporter.

"My charity of choice for that particular show was the Urban Literacy Outreach Program. ULOP does a wonderful job of promoting literacy for every child—even in areas where the school systems don't have enough money to fund extra help for the children struggling to read."

The room had quieted considerably in light of the serious shift in topic. Grayson looked at Jessie, hearing the shift in her voice and sensing an immediate change in her tension level.

The reporter said, "So when you were asked to appear on the reality show Celebrity Challenge for Charity, you agreed to participate in a skydiving stunt. Is that correct?"

"Yes," Jessie said stiffly.

"When the shoot didn't open and the video got national attention, over a half a million dollars was raised for your charity. And shortly after, your books climbed higher and higher up the charts. What would you say to those who believe it was a planned stunt between you, your publishing house, and the TV show to garner more money for your charity, sell more books, not to mention increase ratings for Celebrity Challenge? That sounds like a victory for everyone."

Grayson had watched that video. A few times. Jessie had jumped tandem with an instructor and their parachute had become tangled. Even though they'd released a backup chute, seeing her collide viciously with the ground had made him lose his dinner. While he certainly wasn't Jessie's number one fan, only an idiot would suggest she'd taken that fall on purpose.

"Well… I'd say the four broken bones in my legs hadn't felt much like a victory at the time. Although I survived. And I'm very grateful for the quick thinking and skilled skydiving instructor who fought to save us."

"That doesn't answer my question." The reporter pressed on. "Was any part of the stunt rigged to fail in order to increase the drama?"

Grayson felt his temper surge. He expected a bold, vicious response from Jessie. In fact, he couldn't wait for her to put the arrogant reporter in her place.

"Absolutely not," Jessie answered. She swallowed, and her breath became unsteady—a complete turnaround from the happy, sexy diva of a few minutes ago.

Grayson tapped his mic to make sure everyone heard what he was going to say loud and clear. "Personally, I'd worry about the IQ of anyone who'd suggest that a person would jump out of an airplane with a shoot rigged to fail. Would you take that chance?"

The reporter looked at him, but didn't answer.

"If so, I'd be happy to arrange an airplane and a tangled shoot for you to wear. Does that sound like something you'd like to do simply to increase your ratings?"

"The question is out there, Mr. Reynolds," the reporter answered. "That's all I'm saying."

"And I'm saying it sounds like an extravagant lie made up by people who like to stir trouble for a living. The theory makes no sense in any way. Financially, why would my publishing house risk the life of a bestselling author to temporarily increase sales for one book? That's not a smart long-term financial move. And I'm fairly certain Celebrity Challenge goes to extreme measures to ensure the safety of all celebrities who appear on the show."

Jessie stared straight ahead, but Grayson glanced at her hands, fisted and white-knuckled against the table. Discreetly, he put a hand on top of hers and squeezed, just hard enough to draw her back. "I can personally ensure that Ms. James has much easier ways to secure funds for a charity than jumping from an airplane. No gambling with loss of life or limb necessary. R and R is always happy to donate to a good cause on behalf of one of our authors."

The crowd cheered his statement. The outlaw had some devoted fans, he'd give her that.

Jessie looked down at his hand that was covering hers. There may have been a hint of a smile, but it was hard to tell through all the hair and makeup.

She leaned into the microphone and gave him a sheepish look. "Are you saying R and R would like to donate some money to my charity?"

And…she was back. He pulled his hand away. Damn woman. Try to be nice and get sucked into donating money.

"Are you saying you'd like to renegotiate your contract, maybe even write a couple more Riders in the Night books?" he said. "I bet your fans would love to hear that."

On second thought, maybe this was working out just fine. "How are your poker skills, outlaw?"

Jessie raised a brow in question. "Folks, unless I'm mistaken, I believe my publisher just challenged me to a poker match."

The audience erupted into cheers.

Grayson smiled. He'd been playing poker with his gramps since he'd been old enough to hold cards. The challenge seemed like harmless fun. And a good way to suggest publicly that she'd write a couple more books. She'd almost have to sign the contract with King of Hearts to get the benefit of their promotions department. Fans didn't care who published the books as long as she wrote them. Grayson threw up his hands like he'd been had. "I never argue with an outlaw."

"Fifty grand to my charity if I win," she said. "A one-book extension if you win." She held out her hand.

Grayson shook her hand, feeling pretty damn pleased with himself.

The moderator approached the microphone and shut down the session.

Jessie walked to the front of the stage and started mingling and signing autographs with the crowd. Lila Kent, Jessie's bulldog of an agent walked up to him and stared.

"You think you pulled something over on her, don't

you? Got her to agree to extend her contract publicly, so she can't back out of it."

"Now Lila," he said, full of mock innocence. "You've known the Reynolds family forever. Does that sound like something I would do?"

"Yeah," she said. "It does. But there's something you should know. Celebrity Challenge isn't the only cable show she's been on." Lila gathered up her things and shoved them into a briefcase. "Celebrity Poker Showdown. Season seven. Check it out."

Jessie chased Lila out of the ballroom. "On a scale of one to screwed, exactly how mad are you?"

Lila halted in her tracks, closed her eyes, and held up a hand. "Don't. Talk. To me."

"I'm sorry," Jessie mumbled like a kid who been caught hiding the whole damn cookie jar in her closet.

"I'm going to the bar." Lila looked at her watch. "I'm going to drink as many Jim Beams as I can hold between now and the book signing."

"You want me to come with you?" Jessie asked.

"No," Lila said. "No, I don't. The things you manage without alcohol in your system frighten me. He's a player."

Which sounded like *play-a*, when Lila said it.

"You just got hustled. We just got hustled into a book extension."

"Not if I win."

"You think people won't be clambering for another book, even if you win?" Lila pointed to the elevator. "Go to your room. Take a nap. Don't answer the phone. Don't drink anything with alcohol in it. Put on something pretty and go to the book signing at seven. I will meet you there, but in the name of all that is fuckin' holy, stay out of trouble."

Lila took about two steps and whipped back around. "And stay away from Grayson Reynolds. The only contact you have with him from now on is through me. You got it?"

Jessie nodded, because she knew better than to do anything else. But she didn't feel like she'd gotten played by Grayson. In fact, when he'd put his hand on hers, she'd felt… well…she wasn't entirely sure what she'd felt, but it hadn't had anything to do with business at all. Perhaps that was the problem.

Someone tapped her shoulder.

"You want to get a drink and talk about this?" Grayson suggested. "We don't have to do the whole poker thing if you don't want to. Lila's probably giving you shit, huh?"

Jessie nodded and pointed to Lila's little backside stalking farther and farther down the long hall toward the bar. "Sorry. My mom says I can't play with you."

Grayson chuckled, and Jessie's body tightened with some sort of muscle memory—a split second reminder of his sultry laugh right before he'd slipped inside her body.

Damn. Lila was right. He was a player. Last year, he'd played her to get sex. This year it was apparently about a contract extension.

"That woman has never been nice enough to any man long enough to have children," he said, looking in the direction Lila disappeared. "Or probably even a date."

She smiled and decided to take Lila's advice. A polite distance was the only safe route to take with Grayson

Reynolds. Her head knew better, but her body responded like a hormonal teenager every time he was near. "Look, I need to get going, but thanks for shutting down that reporter in there. You did a good job of making her look stupid."

"No. She did that all on her own." His expression turned serious, and his gaze connected with hers and held tight. "I saw the video. It wasn't fake, was it?"

Jessie shook her head. "No. It was all too real. I have the X-rays to prove it." She smiled, attempting to lighten the weight of his stare. She also had a multitude of aches and pains that never completely went away, plus sleeping pills to curb the number of times she woke in a cold sweat after having nightmares of the fall over and over again. "Look, if you want to discuss anything else, you need to talk to Lila. She'll work everything out."

It was a dismissal, plain and clear. He nodded, so maybe he understood that any further communication would be through her agent.

"Jessie, I'm taking over for Lauren this weekend. I'll be at all the events she was supposed to attend. The book signing tonight. Then the dinner for the raffle winners afterwards. You're going to see me. It's not going to be a problem for us to have a civil conversation, is it?"

Nope. Because she had no intention of getting close enough to him to ever have another conversation. "Of course not."

Chapter Three

If Bourbon Street suffered a vicious Mardi Gras hangover and vomited a casino, Grayson decided Las Vegas's Masquerade Hotel would be the result. Gargantuan beads and shimmering ribbons decorated every corner of the structure. It was gaudy and tasteless, yet somehow had the same joyful allure of an overdone Christmas tree.

R&R had held a raffle contest and picked five readers to have dinner with authors and cover models. Grayson managed to reserve a large out-of-the-way table at Hnaknak, the hotel's upscale Thai restaurant. Dinner reservations and schmoozing with romance fans wasn't exactly his thing. It was the kind of crap Lauren was good at pulling off.

But there was one benefit to getting stuck with the job. If he strategically handled the seating arrangements, it might give him a few minutes to talk with Jessie and feel her out without Lila Kent hovering in the shadows.

He crossed the lobby and made his way to the conference

room that was hosting R&R's book signing.

Less than five minutes inside the signing, Grayson figured out why he hated romance conferences so much. Circles of women surrounded bare-chested cowboys. Three ladies old enough to know better walked by in spandex and fairy wings. Cameras flashed like strobe lights.

It was a fucking zoo.

And part of that clusterfuck was Jessie. Everyone in the place wanted a signed book and a picture with her. Adding to the craziness was shirtless cover model Stan. The tool hovered next to her as if he was some kind of Adonis inspiration for her book.

After enduring the insanity much too long, he was glad things were beginning to wind down. Grayson needed to escort a few authors and cover models to the restaurant in less than a half hour.

He heard Jessie squeal and her unmistakable laugh. Stan had scooped her up and was flexing his ridiculous muscles and posing while slinging Jessie into different positions. Cameras flashed, and fans laughed and shouted obscenities.

Fake Fabio would not be on the invitation list for dinner tonight.

Grayson turned away and bumped into Lila Kent. Great. As if the zoo hadn't been bad enough already, Jessie's pissed off little piranha had found him.

She nodded toward Jessie. "I've got to say, you guys at R and R work with some great cover models."

"I guess," he grumbled. "But you have to wonder what kind of man walks around half naked at a romance conference."

Lila snickered. "The kind with killer abs and bulked-up

arms. Clothing that chest would be like throwing a blanket over the Mona Lisa. Even I want to lick pudding out of his belly button." She looked up at him. "Did I just say that out loud?"

Grayson smiled. If he wasn't mistaken, Lila Kent was a bit schnockered.

"So how many texts and emails have you gotten about the poker game you proposed to play against Jessie this weekend?" she asked. "Because I had to turn my phone off."

Yeah. So had he. Social media spread news quicker than a brushfire. But he wasn't admitting anything to Lila. "So are you going to let her do it?"

"Do I have a choice?"

"From what I understand, Lila Kent always has a choice in this industry. You don't want her to do it, simply say so."

"And hurt her image by having people think she didn't play a simple poker game for charity. No. You know that's not an option. You were counting on that not to be an option."

Lila wasn't as smart as she thought. He didn't want the profits from another Jessie James book. He wanted Jessie to agree to move her series to King of Hearts Publishing so he could be rid of the whole damn lot of romance authors and millions richer.

"You'll get your extra book," Lila said. "But after the crap you pulled today, whether she wins or loses, you better have a big, fat check prepared for her charity."

"Not that you'll believe me, but I wasn't trying to pull any crap."

Lila narrowed her eyes. "What about a year ago? When you gave her a fake name and talked her into bed. You just being a stand up citizen then, too?"

Stunned that Lila knew about last year's encounter, Grayson simply stared and beat back the instinct to tell the miniature old bat to fuck off. Lila Kent was apparently just schnockered enough. Sober, he didn't think she'd have had the balls to mention it.

"It takes two, Lila." He'd talked Jessie into nothing. The attraction had been mutual from the first moment they'd looked at each other. He wondered what Lila would say about the fact that it was Jessie who'd walked away without so much as a backward glance. "I was trying to help today when someone accused her of wrongdoing. Now I'm the bad guy?"

"I'm not saying you're a bad guy. I've done business with your grandfather for years. R and R has always been a stand up company. But I've never seen your grandfather at a romance convention."

"You wouldn't be seeing me here either, except someone had to fill in for Lauren."

"Then why are there fifty other romance authors here, yet you haven't walked so much as ten feet away from Jessie? That tells me there's something up your sleeve. Whether it's personal or professional I haven't figured out yet. I just want it known that her business goes through me. Got it?"

Grayson watched her turn and wobble a bit as she walked away. He had to get Jessie on board before the contract offer went to Lila. Lila would screw him on general principle. It shouldn't be that hard to get Jessie alone and talk some sense into her. The contract offer from King of Hearts was a solid one. Jessie would make the same money she was making now. Probably more. King of Hearts was *the* powerhouse romance publisher in the States.

He just needed Jessie to be reasonable. She wasn't exactly a rock star. Yet. But with the help of King of Hearts, he could see her career heading in that direction.

He glanced back at her table. The line for her to sign books was still out the door. All the other authors had maybe a handful of people at their tables. He plowed his hands back through his hair. Jessie needed to quit yacking with fans and get her butt to the next event. Obviously, Jessie James was too important to look at a clock. The woman did whatever she wanted, whenever she wanted.

She certainly came and went as she pleased. He'd learned that the hard way. Shaking his head, he walked to the end of Jessie's line to cut it off.

Jessie smiled and signed another book.

Stan leaned over her shoulder and said, "Boss man is in the back of your line. You think he wants an autograph?"

She laughed. "No. I think he's cutting me off. I have another dinner to attend. But I'm betting that screwing around and being late will put a bunch in his corporate tighty-whities, so I'm taking my time." She grinned at Stan and winked. Then she proceeded to pose for shot after shot with fans, chatting and thanking each one personally, even pulling Stan into most of the pictures.

When she finally sat again, Stan whispered in her ear, "How long will your dinner last? The Karaoke Lounge is supposed to be hopping tonight. A bunch of the guys are going. You want to come?"

Not particularly, was her first instinct. She'd been on social overload all day. One of her ankles was still messed up from the skydiving debacle. After wearing heels all day, a warm soak in a bathtub sounded like heaven.

"All I really want is a giant piece of chocolate cake and my bed," she whispered back.

Stan raised both of his handsomely sculpted brows. "You sure it's chocolate you want? You've been licking your chops every time you glance at Reynolds."

She whipped her head in Stan's direction. "Have not."

"Have too," he shot back. "Hey, girl. No judgment here. I see the allure."

"Then you need your eyes checked."

Stan chuckled. "Fine. Then come to karaoke with me. You know I don't like to party without you."

She did know that. In fact, there was a very specific reason Stan used her as arm candy. Years ago, they'd met at a conference and hit it off immediately. Their friendship had flourished through the years, in spite of living in different cities. Jessie had fought hard to get him for the cover of her latest book.

Not only was he a devoted friend, but as cover models went, Stan was money in the bank. He had dark, sexy hair. Gray eyes. Killer smile. A chest like a Viking. Ripped, sculpted muscles.

He was also gay.

But the number of people who knew the truth could be counted on one hand.

Stan was afraid he'd lose work as a cover model if the romance industry knew his sexual orientation. Long ago, Jessie had promised to keep her mouth shut and had never told a soul. Until today when she'd told Lila, Stan had been the only person she'd confided in about her disastrous night with Grayson. The long-standing joke was that they'd be friends forever because they knew way too much crap about each other to ever be enemies.

And honestly, hanging together at conferences was a win-win for both of them. Women more or less left him alone when they were together. And Jessie got to have a great time with a stunningly beautiful man who had no expectations at the end of the night.

Except last year Stan had broken his leg skiing and missed the conference. Jessie had blamed him for the Grayson catastrophe ever since. It never would have happened if Stan had been there to talk some sense into her.

"I've got an idea." She glanced at Stan in between talking to fans. "Why don't you come to dinner with me, and then I'll go to karaoke with you for a while. I've got a long day tomorrow, so I can't stay out too late, but we could check out both events for a little while."

"No way. Reynolds didn't invite me," Stan said. "Plus, I wouldn't want to piss you off if he takes me back to his room this year instead of you."

Jessie mouthed the words, "*kiss my ass*" and wiped a nonexistent eyelash from under her eye with her middle finger.

Stan laughed.

"Come on," she pleaded. "You're my cover model and I'm inviting you. Besides, Lila threatened me with bodily harm if I talked to him again without her around. She says he suckered me into a contract extension today and I was too dumb to realize it."

Stan laughed. "That does sound like Lila. I hope she was a little more tactful than that."

"No." Jessie thought for a second. "That's pretty much exactly what she said. Then she grounded me to my room until the signing."

They both chuckled.

"Fine," he said. "If Reynolds doesn't have a problem with me showing up, I'll go." Stan walked away to pose for pictures, and Jessie continued to sign the last of the autographs.

Someone approached her from behind and leaned close to her ear. At first, she thought Stan had returned.

"Do you think you might be done with this anytime soon?"

No. It was Grayson.

She didn't need to see him to recognize his expensive, fresh scent as he spoke softly in her ear. Plus, the warmth of his breath heated her cheek and caused chill bumps to erupt across her neck.

Then fury erupted in her belly.

He'd invaded her personal space and her body had reacted like she didn't have good sense. Annoyed that the largest part of her simply wanted to turn and breathe him in, she tilted her neck and inched even closer, giving him full access to her neck. "My, my, Stan. You are impatient."

He stood, put a hand under her chin, and twisted her head so that she had no choice but to look up at him. She was quite pleased with the little joke until his gaze almost bore a hole clean through her.

"You're supposed to be at dinner with the raffle winners in five minutes," he said. "Could you move it along?"

"I'll be there as soon as I can. Why don't you go ahead

and Stan and I will be just a few minutes behind."

"Stan?"

"Yeah. Cover models are coming tonight also, correct?"

Grayson looked over with a surly narrowing of his eyes. "Thanks anyway, but I've already invited all the cover models I need."

"But you didn't invite the best looking model at the conference. Trust me, everyone loves him. He's awesome." She winked just to irritate him. "You can thank me later."

Grayson stalked away, grumbling something. Probably a good thing she didn't quite catch what he'd said.

Stan approached a few moments later. "Does Reynolds want me to come?"

"Sure," she lied. But Grayson had a lot of power in the publishing industry. The guilt of putting Stan in Grayson's crosshairs finally got the better of her. "Truthfully, I have no idea what the ass wants. Just forget it. You don't have to go. Hell, I don't even want to go."

"No, it's okay. I'll risk being your Grayson beard, but then you'll owe me. You have to come to the karaoke bar with me tonight." He smiled down at her and tapped her nose. "And sing."

Crap. A horrifying memory of a drunken karaoke-fest from a couple years ago centered in her mind. She sighed. Heavily. "Fine. But I am *so* not singing *I Want Your Sex* with you again."

Chapter Four

"They're here! They're here!" One of the raffle winners at the table bounced in her seat as though a Hollywood super couple had entered the restaurant.

Grayson turned.

Sure enough, larger than life, Stan-the-giant-muscle approached with Jessie hanging from his arm. Something had to be off with the guy. Who walked around wearing a vest and nothing underneath?

Then Grayson turned his focus to Jessie. The women at the table were busy ogling Stan, but his attention was solely on Jessie's short dress and sultry laugh. She definitely had an indefinable "it" factor. The entire room lit up, electrified, when she entered.

Much like a diva working the red carpet, she shook hands and greeted all the guests.

He watched her long enough for his mouth to go dry. Her silky nylons and fuck-me heels were black, and her long, wild hair was even darker. But in between was a shock of blue material that clung to every tight curve of her body.

"Waitress." He held up his whiskey glass and motioned for another round.

He had to hand it to Lila, the plan to brand Jessie as a sexy rebel had been nothing but brilliant. Because sexy clung to Jessie like a tight, silk nightie. And he knew from the precious few hours they'd shared, she had a healthy appetite in the bedroom that had met his own, beat for beat.

Jessie laughed and cocked her hip. The stretchy, blue material clinging to her ass screamed for mercy. No—wait a minute. That was just his dick crying out for another night with the outlaw.

Hell.

There had to be a million willing women in the world, but the one woman who worked him up was the dark and dangerous mind-fuck that was standing like a roadblock in the way of his business deal.

Finally, she acknowledged his presence with a subtle nod.

He motioned to the two empty chairs next to him. "Glad you could make it before dessert."

Stan had circled the table with his cheesy flirting. When he got back to Grayson he held out his hand. "Thank you for having me, Mr. Reynolds."

"My pleasure." But Grayson said the words through gritted teeth. Jessie had snatched the chair furthest away and pushed Stan into the seat in between them. How was he supposed to talk to her with Stan seated in the way?

For the next half hour, Grayson listened quietly while his authors answered endless questions from fawning fans.

He had to admit, the five women who'd won the raffle took their fiction seriously. Calling them super-fans would not have been unreasonable. But when the topic came around to Stan's sexy book covers, Grayson motioned for the waitress again. "Why don't you just leave the bottle? Charge me whatever you want."

His head began to pound when the topic turned to Stan's workout routine. Seriously ladies? Okay, the dude was ripped, but move on. And fake Fabio here—

Never.

Stopped.

Talking.

Someone asked Stan if he was seeing anyone special. Grayson damn near choked on his Johnnie Walker Gold. With muscle-boy's healthy ego, a better question may have been who wasn't he seeing?

Stan wrapped his big, meaty claw around Jessie's hand. "Unfortunately, my work schedule doesn't allow much time for romance. But I have one or two friends I try to get together with as much as possible."

What the fuck?

A slow burn traveled a seething path through Grayson's veins. And this time it sure as shit had nothing to do with the whiskey. He leaned around Stan and let his gaze connect with Jessie's. "I had no idea you and your cover model were such good friends. That's handy. I'm sure there are many *benefits* to that friendly arrangement."

Jessie arched a brow. "You have no idea."

Grayson upended the rest of his whiskey. The outlaw wasn't stupid. He'd accused her of having a *friends with benefits* arrangement with Stan, and she hadn't even tried to deny it.

Instead, she sipped her wine and said matter-of-factly, "The benefit of being able to *work,* again and again, with someone you enjoy so much is extremely handy."

"Ha." Grayson let loose a sarcastic laugh. "Romance isn't my area of expertise, but I figured there must be a new hero and a new model for every one of your books." He had no idea why a solid lump of vengeance had settled in his chest, but it had. "It was my impression that Jessie James never uses the same guy twice for anything."

Stan leaned forward, twisting a little to become a human roadblock between them. "I've got an idea. Who wants to take some pictures with me and Jessie?"

Jessie slammed Stan's big body back in the chair. The heat in her expression could have melted a lesser man. "It's really all about chemistry, isn't it? A less than interesting hero only rates a one-and-done book. But if the hero and heroine connect, maybe a series will develop. Isn't it fascinating how art imitates life?"

Grayson swallowed down the insult. He was pretty sure she'd just implied they had no chemistry. *And* called him less than interesting in writer-speak. Lucky for her they were surrounded by guests, because he was about one whiskey away from calling bullshit.

He remembered her nails taking off the top layer of skin on his back. He remembered her crying out, and it sure as fuck wasn't Stan's name she moaned. And he damn well remembered the way her body trembled and tightened as she came around him.

More than once.

"You're preaching to the choir, honey," he said. "When

the chemistry is boring, the story certainly isn't worth re-peating. No one knows that better than me."

Grayson wanted to yank the words back as soon as they left his mouth. *Way to go, dumbass. You're supposed to be playing nice and smoothing things over.*

Jessie narrowed her eyes, but offered no flip remark in return. She leaned back and stared at the wineglass in her hand.

He'd just fucked himself.

Stan sat quietly in the uncomfortable tension for a couple of minutes before he stood. "I'm going…over there… to see if anyone wants a picture." He touched Jessie's shoulder. "You okay?"

She nodded. "Yeah. But I don't think I'm up for karaoke tonight, if it's okay."

"No problem." Stan gave Jessie a quick kiss on top of her head. "See you in the morning." Then he looked back at Grayson and gave him a cool nod before walking away.

"I've got an early morning," Jessie announced. "Does anyone need a picture or anything signed?"

Grayson watched her paste on a smile, shake a few more hands, and then leave without so much as a glance in his direction.

He wasn't surprised that she completely ignored him. For the most part, he didn't blame her. He felt like a dick, and the chances of talking her into signing any kind of con-tract had just slipped into the ether.

But such a spectacular failure in one direction meant a whole new freedom opened up in another direction. He'd spent a year wondering why Jessie had left without a word. Now that he had nothing more to lose, he intended to find out.

He handed a credit card to the waitress.

Jessie was halfway to the elevators when he caught up with her. He grabbed her wrist and spun her around. "What is your problem?"

"*You* are my problem." She yanked her hand out of his grip. "And as far as tomorrow goes, take your poker game and shove it. No amount of money is worth spending time with you. I'll donate every cent I own before I'll write another book for you."

He pinched the bridge of his nose and tried like hell to rein in his temper. How had things gotten this out of control? Maybe he didn't remember the same highlights of their night together that she did. Because as far as he was concerned, the sex had been pretty damn spectacular until she pulled a Houdini the next morning. If anyone had a right to be pissed, it was him.

"Don't you think this tension between us is a little stupid and immature?" he asked. "We spent one night together a year ago. So what? Now you hate me?"

She looked at him like he'd just spawned a second head. "You really are a son of a bitch, aren't you? The worst part is that you come waltzing in here like you've done nothing wrong, and you expect me to play nice so that you can make more money."

"Excuse me?" He laughed and motioned between then. "Is this is your idea of playing nice?"

"You bet it is." She looked around and lowered her voice. "When I found out you were the CEO of R and R, I could have made all kinds of trouble for you. You lied about who you were, screwed me senseless, and snuck out like a pathetic ass. But did I? No. I honored my contract, wrote the damn books for your company, and worked my ass off to promote them. And I made sure to stay out of your way while I was doing it. I don't think it's too much to ask for you to show me the same courtesy."

What the hell version of the truth had she talked herself into believing?

Screwed her senseless? Snuck out?

He stood absolutely dumbfounded and watched her stalk off.

Again.

She was getting on an elevator when he finally caught up.

A second before the doors closed, he stepped in with her. Luckily, they were alone. "What *the fuck* are you talking about?"

"Just forget it," she murmured. "And quit following me."

The elevator stopped, apparently on the floor where her room was. The doors opened and she moved, but he blocked her exit with an arm across the opened space. "Forgetting doesn't seem to be an option for either of us."

Jessie was bold. Beautiful. Brash at times. Her temper hadn't been a surprise. But the fact that she looked so wounded right now bewildered the hell out of him. The alarm sounded on the elevator from holding the door open too long. He dropped his arm and debated which way to go before stepping out and following her.

She jammed her keycard in her door and cursed when it didn't open. "Go away, Grayson."

He took the card from her hand, turned it around, and slid it back into the lock. The door clicked open. "Jessie, wait.

Why did you accuse me of sneaking out that morning?"

She shook her head, but refused to make eye contact. "Don't play games with me, Grayson. I was there. I remember what happened. I'm not some flaky bimbo that's going to let you twist the truth and get by with it." Now she did look up. "But tell me something. Do you ever consider how a woman feels when she wakes up and finds that she wasn't even worth a simple good-bye kiss?"

The woman was one hundred percent certifiable. Nothing she said followed a straight line of logic. And if she was playing a game, she was damn good at it. "I didn't leave you. I went to get breakfast and… " He closed his eyes and thought back for a minute. A horrible, sinking feeling began to take root. "I left, but I also left a note saying I went to the bakery, and I'd be right back."

Nothing but contempt filled her eyes. "There was no note, Grayson."

"I left it next to your coffee mug. Remember those stupid chocolate croissants you drooled over the night before? The bakery had been closed when we passed by so I went back the next morning."

She shook her head. "All that I know is that I woke up and you were gone. There was no sign that you'd ever been in my room. I just figured— "

"What? That I was an ass? That I had left without even saying good-bye?"

She studied him for a long moment and then nodded. "After the night we'd had… I couldn't believe you'd leave… I thought it had been… "

"Amazing." The word slipped out because there was no other way to describe it. He'd gone to her room half expecting a quick tumble and nothing more. But seeing Jessie naked was like taking a hit from a very dangerous, addictive drug. And being inside of her was *still* an experience he couldn't put ordinary words to. He tilted her chin up. "I was coming back. I swear I was."

She swallowed.

Her breath hitched.

He slid his fingers down the soft skin of her neck and felt her pulse galloping. For a second, he'd thought maybe she believed him. Then she pushed her door open and stepped inside. "Good night, Grayson."

Jessie closed her hotel room door and leaned against it. He'd almost had her. Almost played her again. Apparently she had a mental block when it came to the slick CEO type that looked harmless but made love like a Hell's Angel.

Was he just trying to see how big of an idiot she was? See how many years in a row he could hook up with the idiot writer, spout some lies, and use her like a high paid call girl.

"Nope," she whispered to herself. "Not quite that stupid, Ivy League."

But for a second there, she'd wanted to believe him. She desperately, *desperately* wanted to have an excuse to repeat the night that had changed her definition of mind-blowing sex forever.

He'd carried her into her hotel room and taken her fast and hard against the wall. Even a year later, every time she relived it, her core turned to liquid.

They'd both been out of control and greedy. He hadn't

even pulled out of her before falling back onto the small loveseat and taking her a second time.

And that had been just a warm up.

To this day she had no idea how many times they'd made love. It was hard to count when one orgasm rolled into the next.

But she'd die a slow, painful death before admitting to the ass how often she replayed their sexcapades in her mind.

Every ridiculous thing she'd done over the last year had been an attempt to recreate the high Grayson Reynolds had delivered that night.

Skiing.

Bungee jumping.

Skydiving.

Or maybe she'd just been running from the low when she'd woke and found him gone.

"Dickhead," she grumbled. Either way, she wasn't falling for the old, "*Gee, I left a note, didn't you find it?*" routine.

She yanked off her dress, then let her bra fall to the floor. God, it felt good to get out of those clothes. She pulled her hair back and tugged on a tank top and shorts.

At six a.m. she was meeting the winning members of her "Outlaw's Street Team" in the gym for a pole dancing lesson. She shook her head and smiled. In spite of her bad judgment with Grayson, she'd had a lot of success over the last year. Hundreds of people had joined her fan club, and sales from her books had been more than she'd ever dreamed.

She'd done insane things she'd never hoped to do, and met fun, amazing people she'd never thought to meet. She supposed R&R had a hand in it. Lauren had made sure she had ample advertising in all the right spots. And as far as she knew, Grayson hadn't been directly a part of any of it. Surely she could keep her distance from Ivy League long enough to finish out her contract. If in the future she needed to negotiate with R&R, Lila could take care of it.

She stretched out on the bed and intended to do a few of the exercises that her therapist had recommended to help her leg and ankle, but the day had just been too long. She switched off the light and shut her eyes.

Lost in that first twilight sleep, she barely moved when someone pounded on her door. She ignored it. Probably a lost drunk knocking at the wrong room. It was Vegas after all.

"Jessie. Open up."

Seriously? Was that Grayson's voice? She pulled the covers up over her head. Definitely going to ignore it.

"Jessie, I need to talk to you."

She groaned and threw the covers back. Fumbling for the light, she finally found the switch and stomped to the door. But she sure as hell wasn't opening it. "Grayson? What do you want?"

"You don't believe me, do you?"

She scrubbed her hands up and down her face. "Is this a conversation we really need to have right now?"

"Hell, yes," he said from the other side of the door.

She looked out the peephole. Three women passed behind him. *Great.* That's exactly what she needed. Being branded as the risk-taking bad girl had never bothered her, but she didn't particularly adore the label "slut." If any of the other authors at R&R got wind of their tryst, they'd think her book got preferential treatment and advertising because she'd slept with the CEO. She'd worked much too hard over the years to be slapped with that kind of reputation.

She opened the door and yanked him inside. "You shouldn't be pounding on my door this late at night. People talk, you know."

He ignored what she said as if she hadn't spoken at all. "I didn't sleep with you and sneak out. That's a completely dick move. I'm not saying I never do anything stupid, but I didn't do that." He had two drinks in his hand. "I brought you a…" He turned and looked her up and down. His words faded as his gaze stalled at her hips. "You…uh…you don't have any pants on." He slammed back one of the drinks he was holding.

"I was in bed." Her face flushed hot, but she had on shorts and a tank top. The man had spent the better part of a night inside her body, and it wasn't like she was naked. "What do you want?"

He motioned toward her breasts. "And the bra…thing… is gone too." He swallowed down the second drink and turned away from her. "Maybe you should put some clothes on. Because even when you're dressed, I can't always concentrate. But now, I can't really even remember why I'm here—"

"Maybe you should go to your own room." She wouldn't call him drunk, but he'd had enough that he was soundly buzzed. And now that he'd seen her wearing very little, he was babbling.

The devil on her shoulder said, *Good. Let the jerk see what he'd walked out on.*

A more reasonable part of her brain reminded her that a year had passed since they'd had sex. In fact, a year had passed since she'd had sex with anyone. She'd spent more nights fantasizing about their encounter than not, so perhaps clothes were a good idea.

She rifled through her suitcase and pulled out some jeans and a sweatshirt. "I'm dressed. You can turn around now."

He turned, and his eyes raked over her again. He looked at his watch. "Sorry. I guess it's later than I thought. But I didn't do what you're accusing me of."

"Why does it matter? It is what it is. There's no proof either way. Let's just say there was a note, and you did go get breakfast or whatever. You didn't call. You didn't even walk across the hall to say hello when I was at the R and R offices a few months ago."

"Because I thought you walked out. I was pissed, okay? That night was… really, *really* good. And the fact that you skipped out —"

"I didn't skip out. You did."

"But that's just it," he shot back. "I didn't. I think we had a miscommunication."

"I'll say." She couldn't help the sarcasm because he was right. She didn't believe him. "Whatever, Grayson. I've got an early morning."

He stood quietly for a couple seconds, then shook his finger at her. "Wait a second. I can prove it. Grab your key and follow me."

"No. It's late, and I'm not following you." But if he cared enough to come back and stick to this ridiculous story, she was beginning to wonder if maybe there was some truth to it.

He eyed her room key on the counter, picked it up, and grabbed her hand. "Please. Come with me."

He tugged her out the door, down the hall, and into the elevator. She didn't even have shoes on. If she really wanted to put her foot down and stop, she knew she could have. But as pathetic as it was, she wanted to believe him. And sadder yet was the insane burst of excitement that zinged through her. The kind she hadn't felt since the last time he'd taken her hand and pulled her inside a hotel room.

He swiped a card and pressed the button for the top floor. Apparently Ivy League rated a suite.

The large, beautiful space appeared to have all the amenities of home away from home. A sitting area with a desk, a kitchenette, a bedroom…or maybe two. "Wow. So this is how the other half lives?" She walked to the window and looked out over the spectacular Las Vegas strip. "Nice view."

But when she turned, Grayson had disappeared into a different room. He came back with his laptop.

Okay? Not quite what she thought he had in mind when he manhandled her into his suite. He dropped down at a table and fired up his computer. "Come here."

"Grayson look, if you say you were coming back, I guess I don't have any reason to doubt you."

"Except that you *do* doubt me. And you're always going to wonder. Ah, here it is." He looked up at her. "What was the name of the bakery where you saw the croissants?"

She raised a brow. What on earth? It was a year ago, how was she supposed to… "Ginger's," she said, when the name popped into her head. "It was Ginger's."

Grayson motioned to the computer screen.

Her gaze fell on the balance and she gulped. Probably just an account with his play money, but it was close to a year's earnings for her. He fiddled with some statement files and pointed to the date. Then he pointed to a listing: Ginger's Bakery and Café in the amount of $34.57.

Exactly a year ago.

A wild rush of guilt and relief twisted in her gut.

"I went to get breakfast." He stood and brushed her hair back away from her cheek. "I left a note. And I was coming back."

He hadn't left her. But she'd left him. She looked up into his eyes and for the first time, realized what a huge mistake she'd made. For an entire year, she'd hated him. And then hated herself for still wanting him in spite of it all.

"Oh, Grayson. I don't know what to say." She was barely able to get the words out. "I assumed you snuck out while I was sleeping. I was angry and humiliated, so I packed my things and left."

She'd jumped to a stupid conclusion, and because of it they'd both paid the price. She wanted to touch him, at least put her arms around his neck and apologize. But she settled for laying a hand on his chest. "I'm so sorry, Grayson."

He covered her hand and squeezed. "I'm sorry, too. My stupid pride." He shook his head. "One simple conversation would have fixed everything. I can't imagine what went through your head when you thought I'd left."

"Well, it wasn't good," she admitted with a nervous laugh. "But you inspired a couple of great villains in my books."

He gave her a devilish smile. "I really need to take a closer look at those books of yours, don't I?"

Before she could form a reply, he lowered his mouth to hers and kissed her softly, but the gentle press of his mouth grew increasingly urgent with every second that ticked by.

His hands tangled in her hair and urged her head back.

Tentatively, she slipped her hands around his waist. She was doing the one thing she swore she'd never do again—kiss Grayson Reynolds.

He pressed his tongue through the seam of her lips and began tasting her with long, deep strokes.

Her nerve endings went on high alert, feeling raw and exposed, like someone had burned away the protective top layer. There was whiskey and heat and, *oh God,* just Grayson. It was so, *so* good.

He groaned into her mouth.

The low, rumbling sound twisted her insides. The kiss was far from unpleasant, but it wasn't smart either. It felt like only yesterday that they'd kissed—like this—for hours.

Before they'd made love.

While they'd made love.

After.

Her lips had been tender and raw for days. What she wouldn't give to have a reason for her lips to feel so abused again.

His arms came around her, pulling her tight. Heat poured off of him.

"Christ, the things you do to me." He kissed a path down her neck, and the impressive nudge of his erection pressed into her stomach.

Oh, yeah, she remembered exactly how that felt too. Good enough that if he wanted her again, even for just one night, she'd stay. Pathetic as it was, she knew she'd stay.

He backed her up against the wall, positioned her hands above her head, and grinded against her core while kissing the hell out of her. The night they'd shared had clung to her so vividly she'd been unable to give any other man a chance, but she desperately wanted to give him another one.

He moved his hands down her back, starting at the top of her shoulders and sliding south so that they eventually cupped her ass. "Jesus," he whispered in her ear. "You feel exactly like I remember."

Putting her arms around his neck, she sagged against him. She traced his mouth with her tongue and tugged his bottom lip between her teeth, sucking and nipping with just enough force to make him groan again.

His forehead fell against hers. Breathless and obviously shaken, he said, "That was a blast from the past, huh?"

Her eyes and throat burned. *Holy crap. Please don't let me cry.* She'd never been able to comprehend how he'd walked away so easily. But he hadn't walked away—she had. So what the hell was she supposed to do now?

Grayson pulled back just enough to look at Jessie. Her lips were red. Her eyes dazed. He'd tangled his fingers in her dark hair just long enough to leave it wild and sexy. He wanted so *badly* to press her up against the wall and fuck her. Hard. Just as he'd done a year ago. Then he wanted to take her to bed, get her naked, and wrap his fingers around her hips so that she had no choice but to ride him nice and slow, until they both came so hard they passed out. And then maybe bend her over—

"Grayson. Hello. That's your phone, isn't it?"

He sucked in a breath. "Damn." It was his phone. He walked over to the table and picked it up. His grandfather's picture lit up on the screen.

"Hello."

"Good news, boy. I've spent all day with our lawyers. We've read every word of the King of Hearts contract. If this is really the direction you want to take the company, the offer looks solid."

Grayson turned away from Jessie and walked into the bedroom for a moment of privacy. "You think it's a good move, right? We'll have more flexibility to offer substantial advances to writers we really want to work with."

"That, my boy, is no longer my decision to make. It took forty years and a heart attack to see I needed to step back. I'm just the hired help now," his grandfather teased.

"Sure you are." The hired help that had retired but still owned the majority percentage of R&R. The old man might take a few more vacations, but Grayson knew his grandfather would go to his grave with an earnings report in his hand.

"As long as you get Jessica Jameson to agree to a new contract with King of Hearts, you're several million dollars richer," Gramps said. "But they want an answer next week. Any progress with her yet?"

Oh yeah. But not the kind Gramps meant. "Uh, no. Not quite yet. But I'm working on it. Can I call you in the morning?"

Grayson hung up and walked back into the main room of the suite.

"Everything okay?" she asked.

"Yeah. Sure. Just business. Look, Jessie... " She still looked shell-shocked. And sexy as hell. Full-blown Armageddon broke out inside him. Everything in his body wanted to—very badly—finish what they had started a year ago. But everything in his head knew he'd only made one substantial decision since becoming CEO. That was to sell the romance line.

His grandfather had sacrificed forty years of his life for R&R. The least he could do was pass on one night of sex. If he didn't screw things up by sleeping with Jessie again, maybe they could have an adult discussion and he could convince her to sign the contract. Then they could part ways amicably.

He cleared his throat. "Believe it or not, I didn't bring you up here for a repeat performance of what happened between us a year ago. It was just, when I figured out what happened, I wanted to clear the air. That's all."

"Okay."

She'd said okay. But he could tell by the look on her face that things were far from okay. She was confused. Hell, he was confused. He wanted her. Maybe more than he'd ever wanted anything. Except for that multimillion-dollar contract with King of Hearts and to unload a division in his publishing house that he refused to sink any more money into.

He stepped closer and looked into those big, brown eyes of hers. "I lied about who I was when I met you," he finally said. He wanted to touch her. He even moved his arms as if to cup her face, but ended up jamming his hands in his pockets. "I'm very sorry, but I use my mother's maiden name when I just want to be a normal guy. You'd be surprised how many women only care about sleeping with the Reynolds name. Especially at a romance conference."

She nodded. "No. I get it. You don't need to explain."

"I went to get us breakfast because I wanted to spend more time with you, tell you the truth about who I was. I had no intentions of leaving without explaining. When I got back to the room and found you gone… I'm not going to lie, I was pissed. And my wounded pride is why I never contacted you. It's ridiculous and stupid, but it's the truth."

"Not so stupid," she said. "Or if it was, I'm just as stupid. Because it's the same reason I didn't contact you. But I'm sensing that figuring out the truth doesn't mean we can go back and have a do-over."

"I wish. But, no. I don't think we can." Jessie wasn't stupid, she was preparing for the fatal swing of the blade. So he decided to deliver it.

"A year ago, I wasn't CEO of R and R. My grandfather was grooming me to take over someday, but I didn't make the day-to-day decisions. When he had a heart attack a few months back, he decided to retire. Now that I do make the decisions, I don't think it would be a good idea for us to be involved."

There. He'd said it. He'd done a lot of unpleasant things since stepping in for his grandfather as CEO. He'd reprimanded and fired people, cut budgets, cut authors that had been with the company a long time but just weren't selling well. Still, he couldn't remember a decision he'd regretted more than the one he'd just made.

She watched him for a moment, as if waiting to see if that were really his final word on the matter. "Okay. Yeah. You're probably right." She backed up. "I, um…I should go now." She backed up more and stumbled over the briefcase he had resting against the desk.

He grabbed her arms and pulled her close to keep her from falling. On a sharp inhale, her eyes opened wide. Were he a betting man, he'd wager a year's salary the startled look had nothing to do with her stumble and everything to do with their proximity and the firm hold he had on her.

Because it was exactly why he couldn't manage a logical thought either.

Her eyes dipped to his lips and then returned to his gaze. "Sorry. I'm so clumsy." She pushed at his chest, broke loose, and scurried toward the door.

He followed her. "Jessie, wait. Are we okay here? I'm sorry we didn't have more of a chance—"

"Don't be silly. It was one night, no big deal." She shrugged with a dismissive wave of her hand. "We'd both had a few drinks, which is probably the only reason it happened. Truthfully, I don't even remember the night very well, just that I was alone the next morning…and well…we worked that out, didn't we?"

He narrowed his eyes. Like hell she didn't remember that night. He remembered every kiss, every touch, every stroke, and she damn well remembered it, too. But he didn't suppose pushing the issue now made sense. "So I'll see you tomorrow. I'm planning to have our poker challenge set up for around noon. Is that okay?"

"Text Lila and give her the details." She turned and bolted away from his suite as if it had caught fire.

He let go of the door and stood there while it shut between them. Maybe he'd spent too many years in publishing, because it was hard to miss the symbolism of a closing door in the wake of kissing Jessie James again.

Irony was in full force, too. Why the hell was he standing here feeling as though he'd offer up his left nut for one more night with the very woman he'd avoided for the past year?

Chapter Five

Poker was serious business in Vegas. Grayson hadn't wanted to impose on the real gambling floor of the casino for his bet with Jessie. Plus, he figured she'd have a bunch of fans wanting to hang around and watch. He wasn't sure how serious she'd be taking the game, but from his perspective, they'd mostly be horsing around and putting on a show for her fans.

He'd spoken with Patricia Plimpton, the woman who appeared to have more power than God inside the Masquerade Hotel and Casino. She'd agreed to arrange a spot for their friendly poker game.

Friendly being the key word. He hoped that he and Jessie had taken a large step toward making amends last night. As badly as he'd wanted her to stay, he'd done the right thing and let her go. Because now that she no longer hated his guts, as soon as their poker game was over, he intended to get her alone and discuss the King of Hearts contract.

He stepped into the meeting room that had been transformed into a poker showdown masterpiece. A man in a black suit approached. He looked a little bit funeral director, a little bit mafia lord. "Good morning, Mr. Reynolds. My name is Spencer. I'll be your dealer for the day." Spenser shook hands with Grayson. "I work closely with Ms. Plimpton. If there's anything you need, please let me know."

"Seems like you guys have thought of everything," Grayson answered. "In less than twenty-four hours, Ms. Plimpton has worked magic." Three large screen monitors had been set up so that Jessie's fans could watch more closely. An audio system was being put in place. Workers scurried around putting the finishing touches everywhere.

"We have a saying around here. Whatever Plimpton wants, Plimpton gets." Spencer smiled and walked away.

Grayson was helping test the small microphones he and Jessie would wear during the poker match when he heard her enter the room. He hadn't looked in her direction yet. Didn't need to. Because today, just like a year ago, a low, sultry chuckle penetrated all the chaos, and he knew what he'd find when he turned around—the woman who, for one night, had owned him.

Finally, he turned and saw her. As usual, she was jabbering with attitude and cutting up with her crazy, mismatched posse. He'd been worried that after he'd kissed her and then put the brakes on she might be angry. But everyone appeared in good enough spirits.

Except Lila. Either Lila had a wicked hangover, or her face was incapable of a pleasant expression.

Jessie finally made eye contact and headed his direction. Her long legs were encased in tight, black pants. Why the woman insisted on wearing heels that no sane person could possibly walk in bewildered the hell out of him. Then he noticed every guy in the room standing up and taking notice of her. Or, more specifically, the tight, red shirt that was cut low enough for any asshole with eyes to see more of her than they needed to.

As she got closer, the print on her shirt became readable. Her breasts were covered in dice. The words just under her cleavage read: BLOW ME FOR LUCK!

Grayson shook his head but couldn't help laughing. "All this time, I thought it was an act. The crazy stunts, the clothes. But you really are certifiable."

"Who? Me?" Jessie looked down at the spot where his gaze was clearly focused. "This little old thing? I've had it in the back of my closet for months."

"Somehow, I don't doubt that."

"Come on, Grayson. It's Vegas. Live a little. Take a chance. Do something you wouldn't normally do." She handed him a bag and winked. "Wear something you wouldn't normally wear."

He reached in the bag and pulled out a black T-shirt. It had a ten, a queen, a king, and an ace of hearts on it. But in the spot where a jack should have been, there was a two of clubs. It read: ONE JACK OFF.

He smiled. "Nice. But I don't think I can wear this."

Jessie laughed. "No guts. No glory. Although I figured being a high-powered CEO now, you wouldn't be up for it. Too bad." She pouted. "You were much more fun before your promotion."

Jessie learned the hard way that Grayson Reynolds had a hell of a poker face. And his abs weren't half bad either. Much to her surprise, he'd stood right in front of her and stripped off his crisp and corporate button down and put on the shirt she'd bought him as a joke.

But Grayson's torso was no joke. Under his belly button was the sexiest tattoo she'd ever seen. The phoenix bird's tail feathers lead straight to the promise land. Not that you could tell that from the short few seconds he'd been without a shirt. But her lips remembered every line of ink on his stomach.

Flustered, she cleared her throat and looked around after his impromptu striptease. "Do we have ice water in here?"

Grayson grinned and handed her a bottle of water. But when she went to take it, he held onto it a moment longer than he needed to, then glanced at her low cut shirt. "You bought the shirts, I'm just playing your game."

Yes. He was. And playing it well.

A few minutes later, they were ready to begin. Spencer shushed the crowd and began to explain the rules. She and Grayson sat at the poker table and were given five hundred dollars in poker chips to begin. In the interest of time, they were to play seven rounds of seven-card stud. Minimum ante was fifty dollars.

Grayson was better at poker than she'd have given him credit for. The matches were surprisingly close. Then again, he was in charge of a multimillion dollar publishing house. He'd probably bluffed his way through more than a few negotiations.

Before the sixth round Jessie had been ahead by two hundred dollars, but she'd gotten cocky with her last hand and bluffed with two aces showing. Grayson seemed to have nothing. Nothing but a jack. But when he'd flipped his cards, two more jacks appeared giving him three of a kind.

"Excuse me, outlaw. I think my shirt has a misprint on it." Smiling like he had the whole game sewn up, he pointed to the three jacks in his hand. "I seem to have just enough jacks."

Her über-intelligent comeback was to stick out her tongue.

"Is that your ante for the next game? Because if so, things just got serious."

Since Jessie and Grayson were both wearing mics, the crowd could hear all their banter. After his last comment, her fans laughed and became louder. She was glad he was being a good sport and playing along. The problem was, everyone wanted Grayson to win. Even her die-hard fans were rooting for him because if she lost, she owed everyone another book.

Lila was right. Grayson had suckered her good. She'd bet four or five months' worth of work. The only thing Grayson had to lose was the thirty seconds it took to write out a check.

She looked over at Lila, who merely rolled her eyes and sucked down another Jim Beam. Perhaps all business negotiations were best left to Lila from now on.

"This is it," Spencer announced. "The final showdown. With Team Jessie James at four hundred and seventy-five dollars and Mr. Publisher with five hundred and twenty-five. The player left with the most money at the end of this hand wins the game."

Spencer dealt two cards facedown, and one up to each of them. They both threw in the fifty-dollar ante and continued betting until Spencer was ready to deal the seventh card.

Both had two hundred on the line now. And both had

gotten caught up in the crowd and were talking smack. It was the final round, so betting recklessly had become the name of the game. Jessie decided to stay true to her image — go big or go home.

"I'm all in." She pushed her entire stack of chips to the center of the table.

Grayson shook his head, but then scooted his chips next to hers.

"All right folks, it's winner-takes-all," Spencer announced.

Jessie turned her cards up, hoping her two pair — twos and queens — were enough to win.

Grayson had a pair of jacks and a king showing. If he had either another jack or king, it was over. He sat for a long moment after she showed her cards. Finally, he threw up his hands and announced, "I'm out. I got nothing." He flipped his cards facedown and conceded defeat.

Jessie's bullshit detector went off, but she accepted the win.

The crowd stirred with some cheers and some boos, but everyone had fun and the room was buzzing with excitement. In the midst of the chaos, Jessie reached for Grayson's downturned cards to see what he'd had.

His hand slammed down on hers. "No gloating, outlaw. You won fair and square, but there's no need to embarrass me." He pushed all the cards together and scooted them toward Spencer, making it impossible for her to know the truth. "But the winner buys lunch."

She'd been right in the first place — he had a hell of a poker face. She just wasn't sure hers was holding up so well. "I didn't agree to lunch."

"I just lost fifty grand," he said. "I think the least you can do is buy me a meal."

Chapter Six

More than an hour later, Grayson finally had Jessie to himself. It had taken an evasive maneuver of military proportions to lose Lila. But after a cab ride to the Palms Hotel, he could breathe easy and accomplish a meal and a conversation with Jessie and only Jessie.

"It's really beautiful," she said when they entered the Alize. "The view is just spectacular."

"I couldn't take the insanity at the Masquerade anymore. Doesn't it drive you nuts that you can't get a cup of coffee in peace? People even follow you into the bathroom."

Jessie laughed. "I love it. It's my fifteen minutes of fame. Nobody in the real world recognizes me. Or if they do, they couldn't care less that I'm a writer. All the fans at the conferences make the effort worthwhile."

"If you say so." How anyone could love that kind of insanity was beyond him. "After our poker showdown, I thought some downtime was in order. Maybe even have the chance to talk and catch up on a little business." And to bring up the sale of the romance division. The clock was ticking down.

She lifted a brow and gave him a wicked grin. "Here I thought it might be the personal stuff you wanted to catch up on."

His gaze connected with hers, probably much longer than it should have. Jessie was a stunning combination of sharp angles, dark seduction, and sex. Damned if she wasn't right. Suddenly it was the personal questions he wanted to demand she answer.

Why the hell had she jumped from that airplane? Why hadn't she walked into his office even once over the last year? Most of all, who had she allowed to touch her? Stan? Someone else?

"You okay?" she finally asked.

He pushed the ugly image aside with an angry exhale. "Yeah." He nodded. "Fine." Keeping his head in the game was proving a little harder than he'd anticipated. If anything could get his focus back on business, it would be discussing Lila. "Did you tell Lila that we figured out what happened last year and called a truce?"

Jessie grinned and nodded.

"Thank God. The woman glares at me like I'm planning to carve out your liver and eat it with fava beans. What did she say?"

Jessie was quiet—long enough that he suspected Lila's words hadn't been kind.

"She said that I need to be very careful," Jessie murmured. "She still suspects you have an agenda."

"Lila's a total pain in the ass."

"Grayson!" Jessie scolded him, but laughed at the same time. "Lila's been good to me. She's just trying to keep me from doing something stupid. Again."

"Like sleeping with me?"

She looked out the window and sipped her water. "Probably. Lila sees through me pretty well. Probably knows I can't help wondering *what if*. What if you'd woken me with a kiss and a chocolate croissant? What if we'd made love again and hadn't parted ways hating each other?" Jessie set her glass down and looked at him. "Where would we be now if it had ended that way instead of the way it did?"

A sharp, unexpected stab of regret made him reach for his own water. He'd asked himself that very question a hundred times since last night. But he had no intentions of lying to Jessie just to smooth things over.

"You're not going to like this answer, but I don't think we'd be in a much different place than we are right now."

Her eyes opened wider. "Really? Even if we had parted ways on friendly terms, we wouldn't have seen each other again?"

Christ. That was Jessie. No bullshitting around. "Jess, the night we had together was one I'll never forget, but... "

She glanced away, smoothed her napkin, adjusted her silverware. Anything to avoid eye contact. Finally, she lifted a hand. "You don't have to continue with the 'but.' It's well implied. I know it's stupid, I just thought that maybe... "

She dropped her face in her hands. "I'm so embarrassed," she said. "Lila was right. I met a guy in a bar and invited him to my room. What the hell did I expect?" She finally looked up and touched his hand. "I hated you for the last year, and it was every bit as much my fault as yours. But there's something I want you to know." Her face flushed red. "Despite this whole outlaw image, I have never done anything like that before or since."

He'd silenced the guilt a million times by convincing himself that he'd just been one of many for her.

"I don't sleep around. I never have, Grayson. And I don't want you to think badly of me for jumping into bed with you."

Her brutal honesty settled in his chest like a collapsed lung. He wrapped his hand around hers. "I never thought badly about you."

She raised a brow that undoubtedly said, *sure you haven't.*

"Okay." He chuckled. "I may have tried to make myself feel better by dismissing what we had as a one night stand, but I never thought badly of you. Not for sleeping with me." He tilted his head and conceded, "I was moderately pissed that you ran out the next morning and may have used a few unkind expletives then."

She squeezed his hand. "I'm sorry for whatever dumb role I played in this. But at least going forward, we can work together with no hard feelings, right?"

Everything inside him clamped tight. There wasn't going to be a "going forward." Not personally or professionally. Explaining that was precisely the reason he'd brought her here.

She turned his hand over and stroked her thumb across his palm. "Maybe we should try a do-over of that night without the horrible next morning?"

Holy fuck. Had she just…

Oh yes, she had. He could tell by the look in her eyes.

She'd offered a repeat of their night together. If only she knew how many depraved fantasies he'd had about her she'd be running in the opposite direction instead of offering up a repeat.

The concentration it took to keep his dick under control pretty much chewed up most of his brainpower. For the life of him, he couldn't remember why the hell they were even here.

The waiter approached and waved a bottle of wine next to them. At a temporary loss for words, Grayson motioned for the guy to pour, then quickly downed a glass. He had no idea if the wine was five dollars or five hundred dollars a bottle. Given the fact that they were at Alize, it was likely the latter.

After pouring a second glass of wine, Grayson mustered all the willpower he could possibly scrape together and did the right thing. "You don't want to be with me, Jessie. Not tonight or any other night."

He drank a substantial amount of the second glass before he was able to make eye contact again. "I hurt you once, and maybe that time it was by accident, but the fact is, tonight would end just like it did before. And it wouldn't be a misunderstanding this time."

She looked taken aback "Why do you assume it will end badly?"

"Because I can't sit here and pretend that I believe in the fairy tales you write about."

Her eyes narrowed. She folded her arms across her chest. "I'm not stupid, Grayson. I don't sit around with my head in the clouds and write only about rainbows and happy endings. I get that relationships don't work out for everyone, but everyone should at least get the pleasure of *reading* about a happily ever after. At least until they get one of their own."

And that was the problem. Whether she admitted it or not, she believed in the crap she wrote about. "Why do you write romances, Jessie?"

She hesitated, thinking about it for a moment. "Because it's the best job in the world."

"No. I'm serious."

"So am I," she shot back at him. "Writing about romance is a pretty great gig. For most people, there's nothing in the world that compares to being in love."

"For who? For me? For you? Certainly not for Lila. This happily ever after of yours… Who does it work for? I mean seriously, how many couples stay together and in love for a lifetime. None that I know of."

Without missing a beat, she said, "Really? Lila told me your grandparents have been together forever."

He choked out an insincere laugh. One point for Team Jessie, he supposed. Good ol' Lila. He could always count on her to fuck up a completely logical theory. "Maybe," he conceded. Then he thought about the years following his father's death. And how destroyed his grandparents had been. "They've been together for a long time, true. But I don't think I'd classify their life as one big happily ever after."

Jessie shook her head. "Wow. How did someone like you, who basically has everything—money, cars, wealth, power—come to be so cynical?"

Grayson hesitated, wasn't sure he wanted to go there with her, but then decided what the hell. "It wasn't hard," he began.

He topped off both of their wine glasses. "Let's see,

my mom was a drunk who took off when I was a kid. My dad died in a car crash when I was about ten. I was raised by my workaholic grandfather and socialite grandmother. And don't get me wrong, they've been wonderful to me. But gramps has a motto: People come and go, but money is forever."

Jessie chuckled that low, sexy laugh that went all through him. "Alrighty then. *That* explains a lot."

"Does it?" Was she laughing at his life's creed? "Okay, outlaw, you tell me—how does the wild child of dark and dangerous erotic romance come to believe so strongly in love?"

Jessie picked up her wine and swirled it around, then merely shrugged. There were a million answers in her eyes. Apparently she didn't deem him worthy of even one.

"Come on. I shared. It's your turn. Mommy read you Cinderella one too many times when you were little?"

Her gaze shot to his and he knew he'd struck a nerve. Not a good one.

"Actually, we have more in common than you think. I was mostly raised by my grandma, too. But I guess it was my parents' romance that started it all. I remember watching them. The way they'd look at each other, or share a simple touch, it was beautiful really. They had this cool, amazing marriage."

"Had? As in, the past," he challenged. "So even the fairy tale that started it all didn't work out."

She shifted back in her chair with an expression he couldn't quite read. "My dad was a doctor and did a lot of volunteer work overseas. My mom was a nurse and often traveled with him. One night the little village they were in was attacked by rebels, and they were killed."

"*Jesus*," Grayson said.

Jessie leaned closer, propped her elbows on the table. Close enough for Grayson to see the emotion swimming in her pretty eyes. "I was fairly inconsolable. I cried and cried to my grandma. Told her it wasn't fair God took them both. Finally, she said something that made it tolerable. She said that we were lucky they went together. That neither one of them could have ever survived without the other. And wherever they were, they were still holding and loving each other, and that's what we should be grateful for. I have no idea why that made me feel better, but it did. Probably because I knew it was true. Sometimes I look at pictures of them and I think, how can you not want that? How can anyone not believe in that?"

Grayson shrugged. He didn't believe in it. It was a touching story, but getting shot in a foreign jungle was certainly no happily ever after. And from experience, he knew that neither was leaving behind a child to grow up without parents.

Still, Jessie's rose-colored bubble seemed to be working for her. He had no desire to spend the afternoon poking holes in it. "Maybe it's more a matter that some people are built for that kind of relationship, and some people aren't."

"No." She shook her head adamantly. "Everyone's built for it. It's simply a matter of whether or not you meet the right person. That's what the romances are really about. Finding that one person you love enough to sacrifice for."

Fucking fairy tales. The woman actually *did* believe in fairy tales. He shook his head. "All I know is that running R and R takes more hours in the day than I usually have, and I don't make promises I can't keep."

She smiled "Fair enough."

"Fair enough?" he repeated.

Her easy response should have given him a good amount of relief and a great segue into telling her about the sale of the romance line. Instead, it sort of pissed him off.

"Do you know if the salmon is good here? I'm starving, and once we get back to the Masquerade and the ball, it's going to be chaos," she said. "We probably won't have a chance to eat again."

"Salmon?"

She looked at him over the top of the menu. "It's not good? I could do the chicken."

Did he miss something? How the hell could she shift gears like that? "We were talking about the possibility of repeating what we had a year ago and then… salmon? I'm trying to be honest here."

"I know, and I appreciate it. I'm not stupid, Grayson." Jessie set the menu down. "But if you have something more to say, shoot."

Why was she making this so hard? "I'm trying to be truthful because I don't want to hurt you again. I spend every waking moment working. Not that I ever have the time, but if on occasion I do sleep with a woman, it *is* a one-night stand. I've only been the CEO of R and R for a few months. My grandfather is depending on me. I can't screw this up."

She smiled and touched his hand. "It's a big honor that your grandfather has so much faith in you. R and R is a great publishing house. You should be very proud."

He didn't know what the fuck he was missing here, but something about her response wasn't adding up. "R and R is the one constant thing that has always been there for my family. A few months ago it became my responsibility to make sure it only gets more successful with time. You understand that, right?"

"Of course. No hard feelings. You're a busy guy. I get it." She picked up the menu again.

It was completely illogical, but the nicer she was, the angrier he became. "You get it? That's it?"

Heat began to flush red in her cheeks now. "Yes. I get it. 'I don't date. I'm too busy for a relationship right now. I just broke up with someone and I'm not ready.' Those are classic kiss-offs that mean 'I'm just not that into you.'"

"*That's* what you took away from this conversation?" He'd been fighting a caveman urge with everything below his beltline since he'd walked toward her in the Masquerade yesterday. "You think I'm not that into you?" He leaned close and lowered his voice. "If I didn't want to end up in a Vegas jail, I'd bend you over this table and show you exactly how *into* you I'd like to get. The vision of my hands tangled in that wild damn hair of yours while your lips are wrapped around my dick is branded in my brain like some OCD compulsion that haunts me. Every. Damn. Night."

He grabbed the menu from her hands. "I assure you. *I. Am. Into. You.*"

She sharply sucked in air, but didn't say anything.

"But when I get back to New York, I won't be making arrangements to see you on the weekends because I work every weekend." He tossed the menus off to the side. "I won't be sending cute text messages. I don't have the time. And frankly, I've seen very few relationships that don't end up in heartache."

Jessie was stunned. She swallowed—hard—and tried to get her breathing under control. Normally, she was fairly intuitive when it came to men, but Grayson's mixed signals were like trying to unlock some secret code she didn't have the key to.

It was embarrassing enough that she'd offered herself up so blatantly. But even more embarrassing was how quickly he'd shot her down. She'd tried to be gracious about it.

Then he'd looked like he wanted to swallow her whole as he declared that he was "into" her. Everything in her body had heated and turned to liquid. But just as quickly, he'd told her there was no way they could ever be together.

She was way, *way* over the emotional whiplash. "You know, I just remembered I have another event before the ball tonight. I'd really like to freshen up beforehand. I'm just going to leave and catch a sandwich on the way back."

She kept her tone light and cheerful, but dashed quickly away from the table. Confident he'd need to stay long enough to at least pay for the wine, she headed to the elevator. When the doors opened, she stepped inside and took the first real breath she'd managed since seeing him that morning.

No man had ever made her feel the things that Grayson did. Today she realized it wasn't necessarily just in the bedroom. For some insane reason, she liked being near him. He'd been sweet and funny while they'd played poker. And he was oh-so-easy on the eyes. Every time he kissed her, it felt like she'd stumbled upon the missing link.

Unfortunately, he was also a mental case.

She'd learned from her parents that great rewards only came from great risks. But the risks were beginning to take a toll. After becoming smitten with Mr. Emotionally Unavailable and participating in Dr. Death's school of skydiving, she was beginning to see the line between risk and stupidity.

She stepped off the elevator and almost made it to the door of the hotel before she heard his voice. "Jessie wait."

Seriously?

"Jessie, please." Grayson caught up with her.

Against every natural instinct, she turned and looked at him.

"Can we talk as we walk back to the Masquerade?" he asked.

"Look Grayson, you wanted to be honest with me, let me return the favor. I have no idea what you want from me. At first, I thought it might be a contract extension, until you threw that poker game today. Please don't try to deny it."

He didn't, so she knew it was true. "Okay. So I concluded that if business wasn't what you're interested in, maybe it was personal. Apparently I was wrong again. I don't know how to play these games…"

He put his hand under her chin and tilted her face up. His lips came down on hers so fast she couldn't have objected if she'd wanted to. Not that she wanted to.

No wait, she did want to object.

Kind of.

But his fingers moved through her hair, and he groaned. His tongue swept into her mouth with such deep and intimate strokes that her head reeled and her breasts ached. She put her arms around his neck.

Grayson's lips were a powerful and pleasurable head

rush, they had been from the first moment she'd tasted him.

Her breath rushed out when he started kissing her neck.

"You have no idea how badly I want you," he murmured.

She pulled his mouth to hers again. The tight press of his body told her he wanted her just as badly as she wanted him. "Come back to my room, Grayson," she whispered against his ear.

He pushed her away and bent over with his hands on his knees and his breath rushing in and out. "Fuck."

"Grayson? What's wrong? Are you okay?"

"Do I look okay?" He stood and pinched the bridge of his nose. "I shouldn't have done that. It was a huge mistake. I'm sorry." His voice was impatient and gruff. "Come on. Let's get a cab back to the Masquerade. We have things to discuss."

He moved toward the door of the Palms Hotel, but she stood her ground. When he realized she wasn't following, he turned and looked back. "Are you coming?"

Twice in twenty-four hours he'd kissed her into a puddle and then pushed her away. She reached into her purse, pulled out one of Lila's cards, and tossed it at him. "If you have anything else to discuss, discuss it with my agent."

"Jessie, come on."

Nope. She turned and hightailed it in the opposite direction. From now on, she was incommunicado with Ivy League. At least verbally. She did, however, have one more thing to say. But she used her middle finger to do it.

Chapter Seven

Jessie sat with Stan at a beautiful table, in a stunning ball-room, waiting for some of Stan's gorgeous buddies to arrive. She had on a killer dress with killer heels. Stan looked sinfully *GQ* in his suit. The bar was flowing freely. The music was pumping.

And man, oh, man, all she could think about was getting back to her room, packing up, and heading home first thing in the morning. "I must be getting too old for these crazy party nights."

Stan put his hand, palm up, on the table in front of her. She looked down and laid her hand on top of his. In their age old ritual, they laced their fingers together.

"You're not old, honey. But I think you've finally met a guy you don't know how to shake," he said. "And it didn't help when you figured out he's not quite the ass you thought he was."

"Not an ass? Are you kidding me? The guy is a serious

Jekyll and Hyde nut job. You should have seen the way he kissed me today. And then just as quickly"—she snapped her fingers—"tossed me back like I was kryptonite."

Jessie looked down at the red, frothy drink Stan had set in front of her and wrinkled her nose. "This is not tequila."

"No. It's not," he said. "I brought you punch. The music has barely started and you're already two shots in the hole. Let's pace ourselves, shall we?"

She narrowed her eyes. "I'm a grown woman. Since when do you care what I drink?"

"Since the last time you were at this conference, had too much to drink, and slept with your boss." He pushed the punch closer. "Then blamed me for not stopping you. Despite the fact I was in another state at the time."

"Ha." She swirled the punch around and smelled it. "No need to worry this year. I wouldn't sleep with that arrogant ass again if he wielded the last perfect penis in the free world."

Stan's eyes widened with interest. "Perfect huh? Care to share? Exactly how perfect was it?"

Perfect enough that it felt much like someone had put jumper cables up her dress and proceeded to zap her with a very pleasurable electric current. She shrugged. "Meh."

"Sure." Stan laughed. "I'm sure it was excruciatingly boring. That's why you've been running around like Cher's stunt double for the last year."

"I have not." She slugged him in his big muscular shoulder. "Have I?"

Stan raised a brow. "You can kid yourself if you want to, but I've watched you do one asinine thing after another over the last year to avoid dealing with Grayson. Both of you are handling this like ten-year-olds. You might want to consider that he's a little twisted up about the crazy vibe between the two of you, also."

Jessie shook her head. "There's no vibe. Just a huge, embarrassing mistake."

"Okey-dokey. I'll just sit here and pretend the sparks between you two aren't singeing my handsome and highly paid flesh."

Jessie laughed. "What are you talking about?"

"I'm talking about the fact that your embarrassing mistake walked through the door a couple of minutes ago and hasn't stopped giving me the death glare since. I have a photo shoot in two days. If he comes after me, I'm pushing you between us."

How had everything turned to shit in less than forty-eight hours? Grayson had confidently walked in the Masquerade that weekend with a solid plan: to sell the romance line. Things were a hell of a lot easier when he was angry with Jessie. Because once they had gotten past their misunderstanding, he realized he liked her. A hell of a lot more than he should.

The heat from last year sparked again, almost the second he'd laid eyes on her. Judging by her invitation that afternoon, the feeling was mutual. But he couldn't very well sleep with her and then say, "By the way, I'm selling the romance division, see you around."

He might be an ass, but he wasn't that big of an ass. He had no desire to hurt her. Which was the only reason he hadn't gone back to her room this afternoon and shown her that their night together last year had been just a small taste of what he was truly capable of.

Now, telling her about the sale of the romance line and then expecting her to still want to be with him didn't seem likely. But at least it would be truthful. And that was a decision he could live with. Her anger he could live with. God only knew why, but the look of hurt and disappointment he'd seen on her face last night was not something he could stomach being responsible for.

And to make things worse, now he had a niggling in his conscious. An annoying little fission of doubt as to why he'd been so hell-bent to sell to King of Hearts. Was it because Jessie was the number one selling romance author at R&R? And because he'd spent so much time resenting her?

No. That he refused to believe. He had a better head for business than that. That wasn't why he'd made the decision to sell to King of Hearts. The decision to sell was completely justifiable. Romance sales were soft. Romance wasn't a genre he wanted in Reynolds & Reynolds. Plus, if his grandfather hadn't agreed with the decision, he'd have certainly said so.

Wouldn't he?

Christ.

All that Grayson knew for sure was that he was walking into the ballroom, finding Jessie, and leveling with her. He wanted to make her understand that signing with King of Hearts would be as beneficial for her as it was for him. Whatever bridge blew up after that, he'd deal with as it came. Unenthusiastically, he strolled into the ballroom and looked around. He moved from one area to another, finally did a double take when he spotted Muscle Man Stan holding the hand of the dark-haired woman next to him. What in the name of God? His breath jammed like someone lodged a cork in his windpipe. The woman with Stan was in a dress that, from behind, made her look naked from the ass up. There was no doubt in his mind that the long, sleek back belonged to the outlaw.

That damn dress should be outlawed.

She turned enough so that he could see the front of her. It was one of those fancy halter type things that cupped her chest but left enough cleavage for every guy in the room to fantasize about running his tongue through the hot little valley between her breasts.

Or maybe that was just his fantasy.

But he doubted it. Because her buddy Stan put a hand on the small of her back and leaned close enough to whisper something in her ear.

Grayson walked to the bar and ordered a whiskey straight up. The plan had been to stay stone sober tonight and finally talk to her like a rational adult. That was going to prove a hell of a challenge with his tongue tied in a knot. He stood at the bar for a minute waiting for the numbing effects of the whiskey to kick in a little.

Or a lot.

Because he wanted to snap pretty boy's hand off, since it was resting on Jessie's bare skin. He wanted to put his coat around her to cover everything from her shoulder blades to her ass. But most of all, he wanted to take her upstairs and…

Damn it.

"Another?" the bartender asked. Grayson hesitated, but then shook his head. Tonight he needed to keep his thoughts clear and get his brain in the game. Tonight needed to be about business and nothing else.

Game face on, he approached Jessie and Stan from behind. No big deal. Just another business negotiation. As he got closer he saw her hair pulled up in some fancy do that left little curls dangling next to her ears. Her skin was covered in some glittery lotion. How the hell had she gotten lotion in the middle of her back like that?

Probably Stan.

It was ridiculous and childish, but the thought that Stan had put lotion on her back made him want to lose his mind. She obviously liked Stan, as a consolation prize maybe. Because unless he was very mistaken, the night they'd shared a year ago had been front and center on both of their minds. It was obvious in the way she'd kissed him. Hell, she'd invited him back to her room this afternoon. Had she come back to the Masquerade and invited Stan to her room just to fill the void?

Grayson stopped a few feet from them and took a couple of deep breaths. He rolled his head from side to side and reined in the urge to grab pretty boy around the throat.

"Nice dress," he finally said.

Stan and Jessie both turned and looked at him.

"I was wondering if maybe I could get a few minutes with you." He glanced at Jessie and Stan's linked hands. "Alone. I never did get to finish speaking with you."

Stan jerked his hand away and took a step back. But Jessie unleashed a big, fake smile. "I'm sorry. Stan was just getting ready to take me to the dance floor, weren't you Stan?"

"No, no, that's okay. If you two need to—*ompft*," Stan grunted when Jessie caught him in the gut with her elbow. "Okay... I guess we're gonna dance."

The Party Anthem song began, and a gaggle of women surrounded Jessie. Grayson recognized most of them from the poker game.

"Come on, outlaw," one of them said. "It's not a party until you groove." A couple of women caught Jessie by the arms and pulled her away.

She looked back and shrugged, but ended up in the middle of the dance floor.

Grayson looked over at Stan. "You'll treat her well?" It was more of a warning than a question. "I know she's not very happy with me. After I talk to her, she's probably going to be even less happy. Take good care of her, okay?"

Stan grinned. "I've treated her like a queen for the last seven or eight years."

What the hell was that supposed to mean?

Stan stepped closer to Grayson. "I have a partner."

It was loud with the music pumping. Everyone was talking and dancing. Grayson wasn't exactly sure what Stan had said. He leaned a little closer. "What?"

"Jessie is my best friend. I love her, but not like you think. I'm with someone. I have a partner," Stan said again. "But that's not common knowledge, and I'd like to keep it that way."

It took a minute, but then the full impact of what Jessie's friend had just confessed hit home. "No shit?" Stunned, the question slipped out before Grayson thought better of it.

"No shit." Stan smiled, but then his expression turned much more serious. "I'm not the one she's hung up on. I won't be the one hurting her."

Once again, Grayson felt like a huge ass. Which had pretty much been the theme of the weekend. He should have just tattooed *dickhead* across his forehead before he stepped on the plane Friday. "I sorry. I shouldn't have implied—"

"It's fine. A lot of people think Jessie and I have more going on than friendship. She doesn't deny it for my sake. I've always been worried that authors wouldn't want an openly gay model on the front of their books." Now Stan's tone turned dangerously close to a warning. "But I think it's time a select few knew the truth. I've never seen her like this over someone before."

Grayson felt the implication of Stan's words press heavily on his conscience. If he were being honest, he'd never felt like this over a woman before, either. He had no idea what was going on between them. What he did know was that he was ridiculously relieved that Jessie and Stan were just friends.

Now more than ever he wanted to take a shot at making things right. He had no fucking clue how to do that, couldn't even decide which disaster—personal or professional—he should try to fix first. But leaving tomorrow with things as they were right now felt wrong.

He looked over at the crowded floor and watched Jessie dance. She knew how to move and looked good doing it. Grooving from one person to the next, she danced and laughed and chatted with fans.

An ache started low in his stomach. It grew and spread the longer he watched her. Jessie was beautiful. That may have been what initially drew people, but he glanced at Stan and realized it was something much deeper that kept everyone so captivated by her.

Grayson leaned a little closer to Stan. "Just so you know, no matter what happens with Jessie, I'd never talk about someone else's personal life. It's no one's business."

"Thank you." Stan held his hand out for Grayson to shake. "I appreciate that."

"So," Grayson said. "You think she's really into me?"

"Pretty sure. Yeah." Stan chuckled. "But that doesn't mean she isn't going to give you hell."

Chapter Eight

The upbeat song ended and Jessie decided she'd had more than enough dancing for one night. The thing about beautiful, high-heeled shoes was they often made her feet hurt like hell. But the pair she had on tonight was a particularly special brand of torture.

She turned to find Stan and plowed squarely into Grayson's chest.

"Do you have room for me on your dance card?" he asked.

"No." She moved to step around him.

"Please." He gently took hold of her arm. "One song. Then I promise to go away if that's what you want."

"I'm sorry, Grayson. Stan is waiting for me." She figured Stan had used her plenty of times to deter an unwanted advance from a woman. Paybacks were a bitch.

"Really?" Ivy League looked amused. "So, this thing with you and Stan, is it serious?"

She narrowed her eyes. "Maybe…"

Grayson was all but laughing.

She had a feeling the jig was up. Stan and his big mouth. "What did he tell you?"

"Enough. Let's just say I like Stan a hell of a lot more now than I did an hour ago. And actually," Grayson said, reaching for her hand. "I just got his blessing. He's the one who sent me over here."

She looked over at the table she'd been sharing with Stan. Stan waved and gave her a big, goofy thumbs-up. Seriously? Just wait until she got a hold of him.

"One dance. You can be rid of me in three minutes. Probably less now."

"My feet hurt."

He looked down. "I can see why. Those are stilts, not shoes. You know that, right? We could go get some drinks. Sit down. Talk."

"Fine," she said. "One dance. Then we're done."

Grayson took her hand. He led her to the middle of the dance floor and pulled her close.

She immediately debated the wisdom of it. More than once this weekend, she'd made a fool of herself, but try as she might, her body still wasn't capable of pulling off a harmless, meaningless embrace with Grayson. As soon as she inhaled his cologne, her breath caught and her heart pounded against the wall of her chest.

His hands were warm and gentle against the bare skin of her back. To avoid looking in his eyes, she turned her head and rested it against his chest. But then she could feel each breath he took, every shift of his body.

Against all logic, she slipped her arms further under his

jacket, around his waist. In the dim light and soft music, they moved and held each other.

He squeezed her tighter, and it became a struggle to even breathe correctly. Then he buried his nose in the curve of her neck and inhaled her. The intimacy of the act made her whole body tremble.

This is exactly how they'd gotten into trouble last year. A couple of drinks. An intimate dance. A warm buzz flowing through her. Only this year she was pretty sure it wasn't alcohol induced. For the most part, she'd stuck with the punch.

Yet, the whole thing was stirring emotions she'd been trying to put to rest for a long time. The last thing she needed was to get caught in the same dangerous black hole that had sucked her in a year ago.

She lifted her head from his chest and looked up at him. "What are we doing?"

"I think it's called dancing." He smiled, but she didn't appreciate the joke.

"I think we've been dancing around each other since yesterday. I don't want to do it anymore."

They both stilled.

"I know. I owe you an apology after what happened earlier. And an explanation," he said. "Let's get something to drink and find a private place to talk. Please."

It was one of those decisions she instantly knew she was going to regret. But she wanted an explanation, he owed her that much. She nodded.

Grayson took her hand again and led her to the bar, then out of the ballroom, and down a hallway. Just as they rounded a corner, a heard of bizarrely dressed people nearly mowed them down. The man who bumped Jessie sported a mustache, beard, and a spectacularly short mini skirt.

Grayson had a drink in one hand but managed to catch her around the waist with his other. "Are you okay?"

"Yeah, I'm fine." Jessie laughed. "But I think I spilled most of my punch on him."

"Good." Grayson took a few steps and gaped at the odd cluster of people disappearing down the hallway. "Seriously. What the fuck was that? Did you see the dress that asshole had on?"

"Kind of hard to miss, and his shoes weren't half bad either," she answered. "He could give lessons to Scully about running in heels."

Grayson shook his head and looked at her. "Fucking Vegas. The least he could do is shave his beard if he's going to wear a mini skirt."

"Yeah, but his legs looked amazing. Clearly great shoes can make even a man's spindly legs sexy."

"If you say so." Grayson rolled his eyes, and wiped the punch from her hand with a napkin. He led her to an unused meeting room and peeked inside, then proceeded to take her through the darkness and out onto a small balcony that held a handful of tables and chairs.

She walked to the edge and took in the view. She could see the spectacular Masquerade fountain. A bit farther away, the Vegas strip glowed with its never-ending light show. "I hesitate to ask this, but how did you know this balcony exists?"

He chuckled. "You think this is where I bring all my dates?"

"I have no idea what to think about you."

He moved closer and took the drink from her hand and set it on a table. "I had lunch in this meeting room on Friday. I stepped outside to make a phone call, *alone*, and I thought the view was pretty cool. Does that answer your question, Ms. Cynical?"

"Says the man who freely admits to not believing in dating, romance, or love."

The shot was well on target. His face sobered. "That's not exactly what I said."

"Yes. It is."

"Okay, it's not exactly what I meant. It's not that I've never dated. I enjoy going out, being with women who have similar ambitions, who put their careers first. I've just never particularly seen myself as the long-term relationship guy. With the hours I keep at work, it wouldn't really be fair."

He eased her back against a table and lifted her to sit on top of it. Then he pulled out a chair, sat, and moved her feet into his lap. "Why on earth would you torture yourself by wearing these?"

"Duh. Because they're sexy."

Grayson chuckled, then unbuckled the strap from her ankle and slid the shoe off. "You're right. I find it incredibly hot when a woman hobbles out of a ballroom as if the soles of her feet are on fire."

She laughed but poked him in the belly with her toe for good measure. The slide of his fingers on the bottom of her foot almost made her choke on the punch. She thought the fresh air might help the dizzy spin of her head, but so far, not so much. Especially not when he stroked her foot like that.

"My grandfather had a heart attack a few months back."

His comment seemed rather out of the blue, but she hoped it was leading somewhere. "I know. I'm sorry."

"The man has literally worked twelve hour days, six days a week since I've been old enough to understand what working is. I had no idea until I took over. The amount of work is insane. Even last year, when I was going to conferences and screwing around, I still didn't get it."

He looked up. "And no, I don't mean screwing around literally. I'm not in the habit of randomly sleeping around either."

"Could have fooled me," she teased.

"Yes. Well, you're an exception." He unstrapped the shoe on her other foot and began rubbing it too. "The exception to just about everything I'm figuring out."

He could claim whatever he liked about no romance in his life, but something told her that hers were not the first feet he'd worked this magic on. The man had brilliant hands. Of course she knew that already. Memories of all the different ways he'd used them on her rose to the surface. She swallowed down the embarrassment and looked at him.

Their gazes connected and held. The intensity of his stare was enough to cause a momentary stunning of her senses. There was a slit in her long black dress almost up to her hip. He bunched the material to the side and out of his way. Then proceeded to massage her feet and legs.

Her eyes nearly rolled back in her head. "You have no idea how amazing that feels. My feet were killing me."

His eyes lingered on her legs. Finally, he took a deep breath and blew it out, long and slow. "That whole damn dress is killing me." He reached for his drink.

"So," she said, knowing someone needed to get them back on track and quickly. "You feel that it's your obligation to work twelve hour days, six days a week until you're ready to keel over from a heart attack, too. Thereby eliminating a meaningful relationship as a possibility from your life."

He chuckled. "It's not quite that simple, Dr. Freud."

"Perhaps it should be," she answered. "There are these new inventions called personal assistants. Maybe you've heard of them. A good one could probably turn your twelve-hour day into a ten-hour day. Maybe even six days a week into five. Then you're just an average millionaire who has time to enjoy being disgustingly rich."

He grinned and shook his head. "You've got a happy ending for everything, don't you? But in my world, it's not that easy." When he looked up, she saw his resigned expression. "I'm not sure my grandfather or I know how to do anything but run a business. It's just who we are."

No. It wasn't. The man who'd sworn off love and romance like it was a deadly sin was gently and tenderly rubbing her feet. She didn't know what kind of man his grandfather was, but Grayson had needs that went far beyond the boardroom. She'd seen those needs. Hell, she'd been one of those needs.

He ran his fingertips down her shin. "Damn woman, your ankle is even swollen."

"Yeah, but that's not from the shoes. It's from the skydiving."

He looked up, and his whole demeanor shifted. "Why the hell would you jump out of an airplane, anyway?"

She shrugged. "Why not. It was for a good cause."

He sat perfectly still for a long moment. "It was a dumb risk to take."

"Yeah, well. Business is your specialty. Dumb risks are apparently mine. Sometimes the dumb risks turn out pretty spectacular." Like the night they'd spent together. His gaze met hers, and she was certain he knew exactly what she was referring to, but neither one of them dared to acknowledge it. She shrugged. "Then sometimes, you just get a broken leg. But if you don't gamble, you don't get a payoff."

"You don't get killed either." His hands stilled on her calves. "I was in my office when gramps plowed through the door and said you'd been in an accident. It was two days after we released your second book. I pulled up the video clip of the jump on my computer. At the time, we didn't know how badly you were hurt or if you were even still alive. It took us hours to find out where you were and what had happened."

"Yeah," she said a little breathlessly, because his hands had slid to her knees now. "It wasn't one of my favorite days either."

He rolled her thigh-high stocking down below her knee. "Is this where you had the surgery?"

Unable to find her voice, she nodded.

He leaned over and kissed her scar.

That was it. Her resolve melted right along with all her other girl parts. She put her hands on his cheeks and pulled his lips against hers.

Using the long slit in her dress, he pushed the material to the side, then scooted her from the table and onto his lap. His hands moved against her back as if he couldn't touch enough of her skin fast enough. "I can't make you any promises beyond tonight, Jess. So if you're going to walk away, do it now."

There were plenty of reasons why she *should* be walking away, but she didn't give a damn about any of them. If one night was all he could give, one night was what she'd take. "My feet hurt too badly to walk away." She smiled, then brushed her tongue against his lips. "How about you?" she whispered. "Any plans to walk away?"

He had her body shifted and turned so that she straddled his lap before the sentence fully formed on her lips. He really did have good hands. His breath heaved as he murmured, "Not even if someone screamed fire."

She threw her head back and laughed. "Well, if our lives are in mortal danger, I could probably give you a rain check."

"Nope." He ran his hands up her thighs. "Because I'm pretty sure I can come before the smoke inhalation takes me out. And I don't really care about anything else."

She laughed again. "You're terrible."

The convenient slit allowed his hands to continue the erotic exploration of her legs. When he reached her hips his eyes opened wide and he sucked in a breath. "*I'm* terrible. Holy shit. You've got to be kidding me."

Embarrassed, her cheeks flushed hot. "My dress is tight around my ass and this material shows panty lines."

"You really are a bad, *bad* girl. I wondered if your panties would be black. I wondered if they'd be lacy." He put his hand over her bare mound and whispered close to her ear. "If I had known they weren't there at all, I'd have fucked you on that dance floor tonight."

Goose bumps erupted all over her skin. That was the Grayson she'd fantasized about for a long, lonely year—the guy who dared to say things that made her shiver and want like she'd never wanted before. "If you'd asked real nice, I might have let you. That's why I knew we had to get out of there."

He moved his fingers over her, slipped one easily though her wet anticipation. He groaned. "You're fucking killing me here."

She took in a shaky breath and shamelessly rocked

against his hand. It had been a long, excruciating dry spell. He was right—this release wasn't something she could walk away from even if the hotel burned down around them. He stroked a finger deep inside her, sliding and rubbing the one spot that made her body coil and pulse.

He took her mouth again, licked inside the seam of her lips and stroked his tongue against hers, just as expertly as he used his hands.

Her body trembled against him and he swallowed her moans.

She curled into his neck for a moment to recover, but she could feel how hard he was and knew the kind of tension that was pounding through his tight body.

He reached for his drink and threw back the rest of it.

"Anyway you want me. Anything you want," she whispered in his ear. "Take me to your room."

"God, Jessie." Her grabbed her shoulders and put some space between them. "This fucking world hates me."

For a second she panicked, wondered if maybe she'd done something wrong, or if maybe he'd changed his mind. Again. "What's wrong?"

"I'm not having you on this fucking patio because once I get you naked, that's the way you're going to stay for a very long time."

She smiled with relief and stood. Nope. He hadn't changed his mind, he was just debating a location. She put a hand under his chin and tilted it up. "Poor, poor baby. You're going to have to wait a whole seven or eight minutes until we get back to a room to have sex."

"Easy for you to say. You don't have to walk through a ballroom with a dick hard enough to drive nails."

She bent and gave him a soul-searing kiss then held out her hand. "Come on. I think I know a different way to the elevators. My room or yours?"

G rayson trapped Jessie between the door of his suite and his aching hard-on. He ravaged her sexy lips while groping for his key. Why hadn't he dug it out of his pocket while they were in the elevator?

Probably because he'd been preoccupied. Jessie had opened his zipper and stroked him as if it weren't a very real possibility someone could get on the elevators with them. The bulk of his blood supply certainly wasn't coursing through his brain. If it was, he'd put the brakes on long enough to come clean about the sale of the romance division. It was the entire reason he led her to that patio in the first place.

Yeah... Not. Gonna. Happen.

When he managed to open the door, they both stumbled through the threshold like they had a roaring buzz. What the hell was in that punch?

He shoved the door shut and pushed her up against it. The room was black as pitch. The jagged hitch of their combined breaths filtered through the quiet. He trapped her wrists against the cool wood and let his lips travel down her neck. His teeth sank in near the collar of her dress. "This damn dress should be illegal."

"I'm glad you like it."

"That's not what I said. Oh, sure, I like it now. But in that ballroom with a hundred other guys gawking, not so much."

Jessie laughed and holy hell the sound just about did

him in. She unhooked his belt, slid it free from his pants, and tossed it. Everything was taking too long. Normally he'd appreciate a slower seduction, but not tonight. He took her mouth in another frantic kiss and started peeling out of his clothes, tossing his jacket one way, his tie another.

He reached behind Jessie's neck and released the clasp holding up the halter part of her dress. All of the material covering her breasts fell down around her waist.

"Jesus." The room was dark, but the soft glow of the outside lights silhouetted her slim frame. Grayson sucked in a breath and cupped her breasts, letting his fingers play against the hard little peaks. He'd been with beautiful women before, but Jessie had a substantial rack that drove him nuts. He lowered his mouth to her nipple.

"Ah, yes," she groaned. "God, that feels good."

He loved how responsive she was. Loved that she gave as good as she got.

She ripped open his shirt. Buttons clicked as they bounced against the wooden floor of the entryway. "Sorry. Hope it wasn't a favorite."

He lifted her bottom and urged her legs around him as he pinned her against the wall again. He could have come right then and there if he hadn't wanted so desperately to be inside her.

And he wanted to see her, all of her, naked and writhing under his hands like he'd envisioned it so many times over the last year. He carried her a few feet and reached out to turn on the lamp in the foyer.

Jessie bit down on his earlobe and he knocked the fucking lamp to the floor. It shattered around them.

"Uh-oh," she said.

He chuckled. "See. Told you the universe hates me."

"Should we call someone?"

"No. Just keep your feet wrapped around me and off the floor. I've still got my shoes on."

"And you say heroes don't exist."

He managed to turn on the next light without breaking it and then carry Jessie to the couch. He fell back with her still wrapped around him. "It's not heroic, just because I don't want to stop long enough to get you a bandage."

She snickered and stood. "I don't think you give yourself enough credit." Lowering a small zipper on the side of her dress, she wiggled her hips until the material pooled at her feet.

She was naked. And so fucking sexy that his hands shook with anticipation. He fisted them at his side to keep from grabbing her and having the whole thing over before it began.

Jessie knelt, stroked him through his pants, and then slowly tugged down his zipper.

Knowing his judgement was dwindling fast, he managed to pull a condom from his pocket before she climbed on top of him again.

With a devilish smile, she smoothed her hands up his thighs, curled her finger around his waistband, and tugged his pants past his hips and down his legs. Then repeated the slow, torturous process with his underwear.

Sweet Jesus. Her tongue began tracing the lines of his tattoo from under his belly button down close to his cock. "You never did tell me why you have this tattoo."

"It's a phoenix," he managed through gritted teeth.

Breathing heavily, she nuzzled the inked bird and then

traced it with her finger. "I know what it is. What does it mean to you?"

"It means I was nineteen and drunk off my ass. The fucker hurt like a son of a bitch."

She grinned up at him.

"You know what a phoenix symbolizes, right?"

Her brow rose. "Something that rises…" She stopped and threw her head back and laughed. "You've got to be kidding me?"

"Laugh all you want, baby. My phoenix has never failed to rise."

"That is so wrong for a sweet Ivy League boy like you."

He made fast work of the condom, then grabbed her arms and hauled her naked body on top of his until she straddled his lap with their most intimate parts touching. His head was spinning and he wasn't sure why, but the fact that she'd called him "sweet" pissed him off. "Is that how you see me? A sweet, harmless corporate geek?"

Her eyes widened and her breath rushed out. "I…I honestly have no idea what to make of you…*Oh God*," she cried out as he grabbed her hips and slammed inside her.

"Is that what you want, for me to fuck you like a boring, selfish college brat?"

Her arms tightened around him and her teeth sank into his shoulder. "Grayson," she murmured as her breath rushed out again. "I want it to be just like last time."

Which had been fast and furious. Followed by slow and deep. With a round or two of oral sex in between. He flipped their positions and pinned her to the sofa, then drove into her with enough speed and strength to have her body convulsing in seconds.

He stilled when she cried out. What was it about this woman that made him lose his fucking mind? "Christ. You want me to stop?"

"I want you to do so many things," she whispered against his ear. "But stopping isn't one of them."

Chapter Nine

Grayson woke spooned against Jessie's soft behind. His legs were entwined with hers, and his hand was tucked around her breast like he was holding a favorite security blanket.

Her skin was soft everywhere, but her breasts were like warm, smooth velvet. He nuzzled closer and inhaled the scent of her hair.

He thought about how few moments in life were real game changers. The kind that stick and replay over and over—sights, sounds, smells—like a video clip in the brain.

Twenty years later he could close his eyes and go straight to the moment that his grandpa had told him his dad had been killed in a car accident. Every detail, sharp as a snapshot.

Then there was scoring the winning touchdown in the playoffs of his senior year. A moment he'd never forget. Not because they'd won. But because he'd looked up in the stands and seen his grandpa jumping and cheering like he'd never seen the composed old man before or since.

Some moments couldn't easily be classified as good or bad, but you knew they were going to leave a mark. He had a strong suspicion that being buck naked in a Vegas hotel suite with Jessie James was going to leave a hell of a mark. It was most definitely a game changer, because it'd take a severe brain injury or years of senility to wash away the details of last night.

Maybe his basic philosophy on love and romance hadn't changed. But one thing had changed substantially. He wanted to keep seeing Jessie. The thought of never being this close to her again made his gut lurch up into his throat.

Or maybe that was guilt crushing his windpipe. He should have come clean about the sale of the romance division before taking her to bed. But his brain simply checked out whenever she was around.

She moved and her bottom wedged firmly against his dick. He rolled her nipple between his thumb and finger, and she stirred again.

"Mmm." She turned over and put her arm around him. "You're still here. I'll take that as a good sign this time."

"Well it *is* my room. I considered hauling you out into the hallway and leaving you there naked, but it seemed like a lot of work. So I decided to just let you stay."

She tweaked his nipple. "Jerk."

He laughed. "Hey, I was perfectly honest. I told you I was no hero."

"Hmm" She traced a finger over his lips. "After last night, I've decided I'll be the judge of that."

"Yeah. Is that all it takes? A handful of orgasms and I

become a hero?"

"No." She laughed. "The sex certainly doesn't count against you, but surprisingly, it's all the other stuff that make women swoon."

"Like what?"

"Like when you defended me when that reporter was nasty."

"Pffft. Big deal." He rolled his eyes. "Only a romance writer would turn that into something heroic."

She touched her lips to his and softly kissed him. "You kept my virtue in tact by not having sex with me on the patio last night."

"Now actually, that did take willpower of heroic proportions."

She laughed and whispered close to his ear. "And you threw the last hand of poker so I could win." She pulled back and looked at him.

What the hell was she doing? Sex was one thing... "Don't make me out to be something I'm not, Jessie."

"I'm just stating the facts. You seem to have all the makings of at least a hero in training." She propped up on an elbow and ran her fingers back through his hair, then pulled him close and kissed his forehead, his cheeks, his chin.

It was a stupid, non-sexual, meaningless move.

And he hated that he wanted her more now than he wanted his next breath because of it. Hated even more that he didn't deserve this. Didn't deserve her. "Don't do this Jessie. Heroes don't exist, and even if they do, I'm certainly not one."

"You don't have to win a war or save a busload of chil-dren to be a hero. Plenty of women just want a man to put them first once in a while." She wrapped her smooth fingers around his dick and stroked him. "Then we tend to be very grateful creatures."

He rolled on top of her, pinned her arms to the mattress, and kissed her until she had to turn her head and gasp in air.

"As much as I'd like to continue this," she whispered, "I think checkout is at noon."

"What if I said I plan to keep you in this bed for at least another day or two," he murmured as he kissed her neck.

"Really?" She laughed "Have you spoken to the hotel about this plan."

He lifted his head and wiggled his eyebrows. "Money has a funny way of getting check out time extended."

"Well that's great for you, but I need to go to my room and pack. And I have a plane to catch at four."

"I'll have the concierge pack your room and bring your stuff up here." He resumed kissing her neck and tugged her earlobe between his teeth.

She moaned.

"And I know there are other planes you can catch." He nudged her legs apart and wedged himself snuggly against her core. "Please stay." He reached for one of the condoms on the nightstand and quickly rolled it on. Moving gently, he let the slide of his cock against her clit seduce her like a drug. He fucking *loved* the way her body responded. So greedy. So open. And so incredibly wet. "But if you really want me to stop…"

She wrapped a hand around the back of his neck and pulled his mouth to hers. After devouring his lips, she said, "Lila's going to kill me. She still thinks you have ulterior motives for seducing me."

Guilt skipped down his spine and raised the hair on the

back of his neck. He closed his eyes. God, they needed to talk. But his dick was like steel, and she was so damn soft and wet.

"I'm sorry. I shouldn't have said that." She brushed a finger over his lips. "I'll set Lila straight, tell her how wrong she is about you. How wrong we both were about you." She pulled him in for a kiss and then whispered. "I'll stay. I want to stay."

If they hadn't been in that exact position, he didn't know if he'd have chosen sex over a business deal. But right now, any business that needed to be worked through felt a distant second to getting inside her.

He kissed her softly, continuing to grind against her until they were both wet, ready, and nearly frantic from the teasing.

Then he sank deeply inside, but this time with an agonizing amount of restraint.

This time they weren't rushing anything. He wanted to fuck her long and slow until she came undone and cried out for mercy.

Or did he?

The stone that had been lodged in his chest since last night grew heavier when he realized he really didn't just want sex. He wanted to lay claim, making love to her so thoroughly that no one else was ever going to cut it for her again. If that made him a dick, so be it. But Jessie James belonged with him and no one else.

"Grayson," she whispered breathlessly. "Oh God, you've got to move faster. I don't think I can take this."

Still, he kept every thrust deep, but purposely slow. Sliding in and out, time and again. Pushing all of her limits until she gasped.

He opened his eyes and watched her. Her breath trembled out with each thrust. "Come for me, honey." He'd spontaneously combust before coming without her but, damn, she was killing him here.

Her body finally caught fire and pulsed helplessly around him. She screamed. Not his name. Not anything coherent.

Not a chance in hell he could keep up the slow pace any longer. He rocked against her. Fast. Wild. Until his muscles trembled and he poured into her with everything he had.

Jessie had spent an entire night being sexually devastated by a man who didn't believe in love or relationships. Perfect. As far as her life went, it seemed par for the course.

"I feel you thinking." Grayson opened his eyes. "Stop it. Because I'm too tired to keep up."

She glanced at the clock. "It's almost ten. I really need to get dressed and go."

He shifted until they were face to face on the pillow. "But you said you'd stay."

She smiled and touched the rough whiskers on his cheek. "I know. Then I started thinking it's not going to be any easier to leave in a few more hours or another day. Plus, Lila really is going to shoot me if she finds out I spent the night with you again."

"Screw Lila." He propped up on an elbow. "She doesn't have any say about what happens between us. Maybe she takes care of your business, but she can't control who you see."

"No. She's never tried to do anything like that. It's just…" She sat upright in the bed and wrapped a sheet around her. "This is different because the lines blur, and you know it. I think it's important for me to be honest."

Grayson sat up too. "Okay."

"Being with you doesn't feel like casual sex. It doesn't feel like a one-night stand. But I know seeing someone isn't in the cards for you. So I think it might be smart if I go before things go any further."

He took her hand. "You know. Some chick with crazy hair and spiked heels once told me romance was meeting the person you care enough about to sacrifice for." His face sobered "After last night, I'm not at all sure what's in the cards for me. But I think we need to have a serious talk. About everything. Business. Pleasure. All of it. But I'd like a shower and some food first."

"I know I'm starving." She poked his stomach. "I never did get to eat last night."

"Okay, you call room service. Order two of everything on the menu. I'll call the concierge desk and get your things brought up here. Then I'm jumping in the shower. After breakfast we can talk." He leaned close and kissed her cheek. "And maybe do other stuff." He smiled. "Will you stay? At least one more day?"

Hell, yes she wanted to stay. She'd have robbed a bank for him if he'd said pretty please. "Okay."

So the guy who claimed he didn't date had asked to see her again. No use in kidding herself—there was something sort of devastatingly exciting about it. Small time author hooked up with the big time CEO. It made no sense on paper. Then again, some of the greatest love stories never did.

She found a T-shirt of Grayson's and a pair of shorts with a string. It was going to have to do until her clothes and toiletries got brought up from her room. Her curly hair tended to look wild on a good day. But after a long night of sex, with none of the tools to tame it, she was lucky she'd found a rubber band in the desk drawer to subdue it into a fuzzy ponytail.

There was a knock at the suite door. Darn it, Grayson was still in the shower. She walked out of the bedroom and into the living room of the suite. Embarrassment hit her full force. Her dress was in a puddle on the floor. She spotted one of her shoes, but God only knew where the other one was. Grayson's shirt, pants, belt, and socks were strewn about in what looked like a *sex gone crazy* video.

She grabbed up his socks and belt, then noticed the lamp that had fallen and shattered in the foyer. Geesh, they'd made a mess.

Someone knocked again, but louder this time. "Room service."

"Coming." She stuffed his belt and socks behind a pillow, quickly tossed his shirt and pants on the couch with her dress. She opened the door and waved the room service guy inside. The young man pushing the cart looked around, but to his credit, didn't smile or say anything.

He did however stop when he stepped on a shard of the broken lamp. "Would you like me to get housekeeping up here?"

"Oh, uh, yes. I guess so. I'm sorry. It was dark and I

bumped into it." *With my drunken, naked ass while I was having sex with my boss.* "I'll pay for it. You can put it on my room charge. I was in room 495…"

"Not a problem." The kid's face turned red. He threw his hands up like he didn't need to hear any more.

Now her face was scorched hot, too. She'd just admitted this wasn't her room. That probably made a nice impression. And she was dressed in morning-after men's clothing that obviously didn't fit. She might as well of just said, *Yes, I got drunk, naked, and partied like a rock star.*

"I'm sure we have Mr. Reynolds's card on file," he said as he pushed the cart near the dining table. "But I don't think management charges for little things like that." The bellhop bent to pick something up. In his defense, it looked like it could have been one of the white cloth napkins from the food cart. But it turned out to be Grayson's underwear. The young guy quickly dropped them and coughed away a smile. "Is there anything else I can do for you?"

"No. Thank you. Oh, just let me get my purse for your tip." She looked around. Had she dropped it by the door? Or the couch? Maybe she'd carried it in the bedroom…

"You know what. That's really not necessary—"

"No, just a second," she said. She'd mortified the young guy. The least she could do was give him a handful of cash. She picked up Grayson's pants. Surely he'd have a wad of money in his pocket or a wallet or something.

Nope. Pockets as empty as her head.

"Oh. Over here." She spotted his briefcase on the desk. "Let me just look through here, he probably has some money or something—"

"It's okay, really. We'll just put this on his tab. I'll be

around all day if you wish to find me later. You have a nice morning, miss," he said as he backed out the door.

Jessie nodded and looked back down at Grayson's briefcase. She hadn't found his wallet or any money, but there was an envelope with her name on it and the logo from King of Hearts publishing. In fact there were several envelopes with the King of Hearts Logo.

Instinct told her to pick up the one with her name on it, but she shouldn't have been in his briefcase. She was struggling with the moral dilemma when Grayson walked out of the bedroom.

"Hey, is breakfast here? It smells great." He turned and looked at her, noticed her hand on his briefcase. "Is there something you need inside my briefcase?"

She shook her head. "I was looking for cash to tip the delivery guy. I can't find my purse so I picked up your pants hoping to find some money. Then I thought maybe you'd dropped your wallet in your briefcase."

He stepped in front of her. "I put your purse on the nightstand next to you. I figured women like to keep those things close by."

"You know, I'm not really hungry. I think I'll just run down to my room—"

He caught her arm as she turned. "What did you see in my briefcase?"

She considered murmuring "nothing" and escaping. A little white lie would have made things easier. But not giving Grayson the benefit of the doubt last year had been a huge mistake. "An envelope with my name on it. And the King of Hearts logo."

"And?"

"And nothing. I'm standing here trying to figure out why there's an envelope in your briefcase with my name on it and another company's logo. I'm telling myself it's nothing." She looked up at him. "Is it nothing?"

Grayson didn't reply.

"Did they offer to buy my contract or something? If so, you don't have to hide anything. R and R has done a lot for my career. I wouldn't jump ship just for a little more money."

He let go of her arm, walked to the briefcase, and took out the file. "It's a little more complicated than that. Sit down, Jess."

The expression on his face wasn't reassuring. Neither was the fact that he'd asked her to sit. A small chair sat across from the couch they'd made love on. She dropped down on it.

He leaned back against the desk. "King of Hearts has offered to buy the entire romance division of Reynolds and Reynolds."

"Well, that's insane. You're not going to sell to them, are you?"

He was quiet for a long moment. "I'm considering it, yes."

"What? Why? King of Hearts is determined to monopolize the romance industry. R and R does a great romance business and is one of their key competitors. You should be proud of that."

"Romance is what King of Hearts does," he said. "It's what they want to do, and they do it well. I'm not interested in pursuing the romance division any longer."

"Why? Is the romance division losing money?"

"Some. Yes. But not everything is about money, Jessie. I want R and R to be one of the most respected publishing houses out there. I want to do serious literature. I want big names."

"Uh, hello. What am I? Do you know how many books I've signed this weekend? Better yet, do you know how many books I've sold over the last month?"

"Romance is not what I want R and R to be known for."

She propped her hands on her hips and glared at him. "I don't believe this. You really are a romance snob. Not just your personal life, but your business, too. You own one of the most successful publishing houses in the U.S. and you want to ditch the romance line? Even if you don't personally like romance, what kind of sense does that make?"

"It makes perfect sense if you're not interested in offering the same story with the same happily ever after in every book. A couple meet. They have some issue to overcome. One of them makes a big grand gesture and they fall in love. The end."

"Well, that's belittling. You can simplify a formula for every book out there, no matter what the genre is. It's fun to read about love and romance. It makes people happy. It gives them hope."

"It makes people delusional and gives them unrealistic expectations. Nobody rides off into the sunset with a happily ever after. Plus, do you really think you're going to be nominated for a Pulitzer with your next erotic romance?"

That stung. And now she certainly knew how little he thought of her work. "Screw you, Grayson. I'm not trying to change the world. But if I can entertain someone, or take someone's mind off their problems, or maybe give a woman hope that good men are out there and do exist, that's enough for me."

She looked around and finally found her other shoe. "And by the way, the sales from my meager little romances are probably paying R and R's rent so that you can go mine for that one little chunk of gold fiction you think is out there somewhere. Maybe you need to think about that."

"Okay, wait just a second." He put his hands on her arms and guided her back to the chair. "Please sit for a second. You're looking at this all wrong. King of Hearts is good at what they do. The contract they're offering is solid. You'll make more money with them than you would if you stayed with R and R. Their advertising and marketing are amazing. You're going to like it there."

"Well that's not really your call is it? My contract is void if you sell the romance line. And you know it. Lila and I will decide what publishing house we want to be with."

"Jessie, will you wait just a damn minute and be reasonable? Why on earth wouldn't you want to go with King of Hearts? They're chomping at the bit to get you. You could probably negotiate anything in the contract that you don't like. I don't want you upset about this."

"Well, I am upset." She stood and squared off with him. "It pisses me off when people dismiss the romance genre as frivolous when love and relationships are the most basic, important thing in every person's life. Plus, I'm not interested in giving King of Hearts an even bigger monopoly in this industry than they already have. But whatever, do what you have to do and I'll do what I have to do. You can talk to Lila about how to handle this."

"I'd rather talk to you. For five fucking minutes will you sit and hear me out. The author that King of Hearts wants most is you."

The truth finally drilled through the dense stupidity in her head. She swallowed back the bile that had risen in her throat. When the capability to speak returned, she murmured, "Does the sale of the romance division depend on whether or not I sign with King of Hearts?"

His expression was a guilt-stricken look if she'd ever seen one. Her shoes slipped from her fingers. She dropped back into the chair. "You've got to be shitting me. I fell for you. Again." She looked up at him. "You didn't sleep with me because you wanted me. You were trying to soften me so I'd sign with King of Hearts."

He kneeled in front of her. "No, I wouldn't do that. I've been trying to get you alone, to talk to you—"

She held up a hand to stop his lame attempt. "Just answer one question. When you walked into the Masquerade this weekend, what was your main objective for being here? The whole time, have you been trying to figure out how to get me to sign a contract with King of Hearts?"

He stood, then paced across the room. "That is not a fair question." He turned back to her. "Because when I walked into this conference, I thought you had snuck out on me last year. Just like you thought I'd snuck out on you. So yes, I had hopes of clearing the air and discussing the new contract."

"But after, when we figured out the truth. Why didn't you just tell me then?"

"I wanted to. I tried all day Saturday to get a free moment with you." He plowed his fingers back through his hair. "You don't honestly believe that I would seduce you in hopes of getting you to sign a new contract. You may be angry, but give me a little credit. That's ridiculous. I was trying very hard *not* to sleep with you so that we wouldn't have this issue, but last night…"

She studied his expression, trying to find some kind of truth that didn't make her feel used and stupid.

"Is it always like that for you?" Tears stung in her eyes after she'd asked the question, but she had to know. "Was last night typical—"

"No. That's what I'm saying. Last night happened because I wanted you more than I've ever wanted anything. You and me—us—it's off the charts, and it complicates things, I know."

She swiped at the tears, really, *really* wanting to believe last night had meant something to him.

He picked up her hand. "Whatever happens business-wise, it doesn't have to impact whether or not we keep seeing each other."

Sure it did. Because she wasn't at all positive that the most intimate night of her life had been real. She hated the ugly suspicion. But it would be so easy for him to charm her, even for a few more weeks, or maybe a month, until his business deal went through then drop her like the dead weight she'd have become.

"What happens if I don't sign?"

He shrugged. "I'm not sure. I suppose I'll try to renegotiate with King of Hearts. One way or the other, I'm selling the division, Jess. It would be really helpful if you and Lila would just look at the contract and consider signing, too."

It didn't make sense. After last night, she couldn't believe she was looking at the same man. "Why are you doing this?"

"Because the business projections for the next five and ten years tell me where I want to be and how I'd like R and R to be established in the industry. There are a few very valuable authors just hitting their stride. With the overhead from this sale, I'll have the resources to entice them to sign with R and R."

"So this decision is based on a calculated hope that a few random authors will sign with you. But screw the authors that have already worked their asses off to make you successful."

"It's business, Jess. It's not personal."

"The hell it's not. Look me in the eyes and tell me the way we left things last year didn't give you the teeniest, tiniest incentive to screw me and the romance line. Then tell me that I shouldn't take it personally that you value an author you don't even know more than you value the ones who are making you good money right now."

"You're completely incapable of looking at the big picture. Not everything is about you. It's about what is going to affect our bottom line the most over the next ten years."

"Fine. What if I signed a contract that said I'd write more books for R and R? I won't ask for more money or more advertising dollars. You don't just have me, you've got several up and coming romance authors who are hot right now. I know I could get them on board. None of us want to see one less romance publisher out there."

She'd just offered him a hell of a deal. Without Lila's consent or advice. But if he had any respect for her professionally, he wouldn't ask her to write for a publishing house she didn't want to write for. And if he had any real feelings for her personally, he wouldn't be so eager to push her away. "Will you reconsider?"

None of what she way saying was making a dent in his determination, she could tell. He could claim whatever innocence he wanted to, but he'd come here for one reason this weekend and that was to get rid of her *and* the romance division.

"So after last night, after everything I've offered, you still want me to sign that contract? Surely you know I can't write for King of Hearts and date the CEO of R and R."

He didn't answer straightaway. Because of course he knew it. And he'd known it last night, too.

He put a finger under her chin and tilted her head up. God, she was stupid and embarrassed, standing there with tears rolling, praying he was going to agree to give the romance line, and their relationship, a chance.

"It's in everyone's best interest if you go with King of Hearts."

"Okay." She kept her gaze locked with his and choked back the burn in her throat. When Grayson Reynolds decided to fuck you, you certainly knew you had been completely and thoroughly fucked. "Just send the contract to Lila, and I'll sign."

He put his hands on her shoulders "I know you haven't read it yet, but I have. It's a good contract. I promise."

"Okay." She excused herself, went into the restroom, and got dressed. She picked up her purse on the way back to the foyer.

"Damn it, Jessie. So I make one business decision you don't like and you leave. Now you get why I believe people come and people go, but the business is forever. Score one for gramps."

"You know, there's a big difference between people leaving you and you pushing everyone away. You really should crack open one of those romance books you publish and read it. You might be surprised what you'd learn about people taking a real risk once in a while."

He stepped closer to her. "Risks are your specialty, not mine. I never lied to you. I was honest about who I am."

"Yes. You were. I was the one who was wrong. Because I actually thought if we had one more night you'd change your mind about what was important. But now I actually understand who we both are."

"I shouldn't have let last night happen, knowing that we still needed to have this discussion. I'm sorry."

"I'm not. Like you said, stupid risks are my specialty. Calculated business is yours. But now I know you and I are two very different creatures. And that's never going to change."

"Honestly? Are we? We work in the same business. We both work our asses off for success. And have you ever— even once—come close to having what we have in the bedroom with someone else?"

"No. I haven't and that's just it. If someone made me choose between writing another book and being with you, I'd never turn my computer on again." She opened the door to his suite, then reached up and kissed his cheek. "Good-bye, Grayson."

Chapter Ten

"Grayson." A voice penetrated the flashback of Jessie in that damn dress of hers.

"Grayson, are you okay with that?" The guy from the accounting department continued to stare at him.

Grayson cleared his throat and looked around the conference table. "Let me think about it some more, and I'll get back to you tomorrow."

The numbers had started to blur about a half hour ago—right about the same time the accounting manager had shown a PowerPoint of their new business strategy. Jessie's picture popped up on the screen along with the amount of yearly income they estimated losing when she signed with King of Hearts.

"That's enough for today," Grayson's grandfather said. "Everybody take off. We'll email a time to resume this tomorrow."

Grayson sighed and scrubbed his hands up and down his face a couple times. Gramps was about to hand him his ass on a platter. It wasn't like he didn't deserve it. Jessie had been right. He'd been handed money and power. Walked into the position of CEO in a thriving business. Nice car. Hell of a penthouse. Enough cash at the ready to do pretty much anything he wanted to do.

He'd initiated major changes in their publishing house. The whole company had come together to implement how the transition would take place. And he couldn't get his head in the game to save his soul.

After the room cleared, Grayson's grandfather leaned back against the conference table with his hands in his pockets.

Grandpa had a bit of a tan going on. Wearing his golf shirt and khakis, he looked about ten years younger since he'd retired. Of course, he still occupied his office and had been at work more days than not.

"So does she have a name? Or should I be scheduling a CAT scan of your brain?" Gramps said.

"I'm fine."

Gramps laughed. "Really? Because Jeffery in accounting just asked you if you were okay with ordering pizza for the staff luncheon tomorrow, and you told him you needed more time to think about it. If the lunch menu is tripping you up, I'm a little concerned about the multimillion dollar business contract."

Yeah. Grayson was concerned about it, too. He rubbed his forehead. His brain hurt. But probably not half as bad as his pride was going to hurt when he told his grandfather he'd made the mother of all mistakes. "I'm fine. I've just got a few things on my mind."

His grandpa scooted back and sat on top of the table. "I always planned to have a talk with you before making you CEO. When the heart attack happened, I didn't get the chance to, but I think we should have it now."

Grayson sighed. The last thing he needed right now was a lecture. "Look, I was a little distracted today. That's all. Can we call it a day?"

"No, we can't."

With more than a little attitude, Grayson leaned back in his chair. "Fine."

"It occurred to me somewhere around the seventh hole last weekend, that I've never once asked you if you *want* to be CEO of Reynolds and Reynolds."

"Seriously? I get distracted during one stupid meeting, and that means I don't want to be CEO anymore?" Grayson stood. "I don't need this today. I really don't."

Grayson's grandfather stood also. "Sit down, boy."

Grayson hadn't seen that particular brand of heat in his grandfather's eyes in quite some time. Maybe not since he'd gotten thrown out of the college dorms and fined ten grand for making a giant Slip and Slide with a plastic tarp and a beer keg.

So he sat. "I'm sorry. The distractions have nothing to do with whether I want to be CEO or not. I assure you."

"I didn't build this company for you to feel obligated to run it. I built something with a net worth so you could do anything you wanted to with the money. Sell the damn company and buy a Starbucks if that's what appeals to you."

"Gramps—"

"I mean it, Grayson. All I've ever wanted is for you to be happy."

"I am happy."

"It doesn't look like it. Not to me or your grandmother. And after that last conference, you've been moody and distant—"

"It's Jessica Jameson, okay."

Gramps was quiet for a long moment before he spoke. "Jessie James? Our author?"

Grayson nodded.

"Did you sleep with her?"

Grayson nodded again.

"Oh, God. Is she pregnant?"

Grayson looked up. "What? No."

"Suing you for sexual harassment?"

In disbelief, Grayson shook his head. "No. Nothing like that." Somehow he'd made the mistake of thinking that admitting to woman trouble might save him from a long chat about his professional aspirations. Now he was facing the third degree over Jessie.

"She's angry because I'm selling our romance division to King of Hearts. Angry because I didn't take her up on the offer to write more books for us. But I was just being honest. I told her business was always going to come before pleasure. You know that's true. Hell, you've lived it."

Gramps pulled a chair up to the long conference table and folded his hands as he did during so many meetings he'd led. "If I've ever given you the impression that this business was more important to me than you or your grandmother, I'm sorry, Grayson. That wasn't my intent."

"I didn't say that. And I do love this business. But I've

seen how much time you've put in. I know how important it is to be on top of everything—"

"Do you know why I put in so many hours?"

"Because there's a fuckload of work."

"Yes." Gramps laughed. "There is. But no one says you have to do it by yourself."

"You did."

"But I did… Well, I did it because I missed your dad." Gramps looked him in the eye. "There's a kind of pain that goes along with losing a child that is indescribable. My deepest hope is that you never know that kind of pain in your lifetime. The only things that could distract me from it were you and work. You gave us a reason to go on. Your grandmother buried herself in taking care of you. I buried myself in work. It was just how we coped.

Grayson nodded but couldn't quite find his voice. After a long moment he said, "Have you ever read one of Jessie's books."

"Oh, sure. Jessie is one of your grandmother's favorite authors. Sometimes we read them together."

Grayson pinched the bridge of his nose. The sex in Jessie's books could make a sailor blush. That was not information he needed to know. "I spent the last few days reading them, too."

"Yeah? What'd you think?"

Grayson merely shrugged, because heat traveled up his neck like a brushfire. He didn't think anything. He *knew* that the Tessa and Ian love scene was a verbatim reenactment of his first night with Jessie. He knew Jessie had a hell of a talent for sucking you into a story, so deeply you couldn't put the damn book down to save your soul. And he knew, well beyond any shadow of a doubt, that discrediting the stories she loved to tell, and selling the romance line, had been the biggest fucking mistake he'd ever made.

Well…other than letting Jessie walk out of his life for a second time. "What's the dumbest thing you ever did while running R and R?"

"Besides putting my grandson in charge?" Gramps teased. "Relax I'm just joking, boy." Gramps thought on it for a moment. "My biggest mistakes were probably with your grandmother. I paid plenty of attention to the business. I suspect I should have paid more attention to her. Luckily, a good woman who loves you will forgive your mistakes."

"That's good," Grayson said. "Because I think I've made some epic ones."

J essie waited for Lila in front of her Chicago condo. Lila pulled up in her little compact rental car and Jessie folded herself into it.

"You didn't have to rent a car, you know. We have these great new inventions in Chicago. They're called taxis."

"King of Hearts has an office in a building outside of the city. It's an hour or so away. That's where we're headed."

"I thought their corporate offices were in New York, about five minutes from R and R. This whole thing seems weird, don't you think? Why wouldn't we have just done this in New York?"

Lila shrugged. "Publishers have offices all over the world. Plus, I might have mentioned your reluctance ever step foot in the R and R building again. Who knows, maybe King of

Hearts just wants to cater to their favorite new author."

"Mmm," was the only response Jessie could muster.

"Could you at least try not to look like you're going to a funeral? You need to make peace with the fact you write for King of Hearts now. They aren't the enemy."

"No. They're not. Trust me, I know all too well who the enemy is."

"Do you? R and R didn't exactly throw you under a bus. You've gotten a hell of a contract offer out of this."

Jessie nodded. It wasn't R&R, or King of Hearts, or the contract, or the money. It was the fact that Grayson had taken a belief she'd held onto since her parents had died and shattered it all to hell. He was right. Her love-will-conquer-all bullshit was exactly that.

She thought she'd know when sex turned into making love. And when making love turned into something that was about emotion and connection. Turned out it was a little hard to connect with a corporate jack-hole who freely admits to caring more for money and business than people.

And really, as badly as she hated to admit it, Grayson had a point. How many people did she know living the happily ever after? More people probably believed in aliens than love. "After I fulfill this contract, I think I'll try my hand at an alien/horror type of book. What do you think?"

Lila sighed. "I think if I'm lucky, I'll be dead by then. You ever heard of sticking with what you know? No one wants to read about green creatures with antennae bumping uglies. It's wrong. You write sex and love and you're good at it. Don't try to reinvent the wheel because Grayson yanked your chain."

Jessie shook her head, but couldn't help smiling. Most

people thought Lila had a cock-eyed and negative view of the world. It was a bit disturbing how closely Jessie related with her.

"I guess you're right. A new company and a new contract will be good. Let's just sign on the dotted line and get this day over with."

But Jessie's suspicions began to run wild the further they got from the city. "You're not heading into corporate suburbia. I'm not stupid, Lila. What's going on?"

Lila turned onto a road that led to the airstrip where Jessie's skydiving accident had happened.

"Great." Jessie folded her arms, enraged that this had been in the works and no one had told her. "Is this King of Hearts idea? To hold a press conference where I almost killed myself. Wow, they're not going to miss any opportunity to sell a book are they?"

Lila pulled to a stop in front of the skydiving school. Jessie got out and slammed the door. She stalked around to Lila's side of the car. "I know your job is to make us both money. But this is low. You should have told me this is where they wanted to have a press conference. Do you know how hard it was to put this behind me? Reporters are still accusing me of—"

"There's no press conference. Can you just—" Lila made the motion of buttoning her lip. "Be quiet. For a minute or two. Come on."

Jessie firmly held her ground as Lila began to walk. "If you think I won't march straight back to that highway and hitchhike back to the city, you don't know me nearly as well as you think you do. You better spill it—"

"For fuck's sake." Lila whipped around on her. "It's

Grayson. He wanted you here. He planned this. King of Hearts is not coming because Grayson is not selling to them. He decided to keep the romance line and you." Lila threw her hands up in frustration. "Although at this point I'm questioning the logic."

Jessie felt a wild rush of emotion. Her legs began to shake and her eyes burned. A lump swelled in her throat, too large to talk around.

"Jessie, Lila. You're right on time." Grayson Reynolds, Senior, approached them.

Lila held out her hand. "Mr. Reynolds, always good to see you. How are you?"

"Couldn't be better," he said. "With the exception that my grandson is getting ready to jump out of a perfectly good airplane."

Jessie's heart raced. What on earth? Why would he do that? Grayson had scolded her, told her that jumping from an airplane had been a dumb risk. Considering how many months of therapy she'd endured to walk correctly again, she tended to agree.

"Why is he doing this?" Jessie asked.

Grayson's grandpa shrugged. "I'm not sure. He mumbled something about taking a risk. Learning to live a little."

"This is completely ridiculous. Where is he?" Jessie stomped toward the building where the classes took place. "Wait until I get my hands on that ass, I'm going to…" She stopped, drew in a breath, and glanced at Lila. She'd just called the grandson of one of the most respected names in publishing an ass. "Sorry."

"Hey." Grayson's granddad put his hands up in defense. "I've been married for forty-five years. I know that look. I'm not about to get in your way of you going after the ass. But his plane took off a few minutes ago so you're going to have to wait until he parachutes down."

Jessie rounded the building and hanger. She looked up and saw Grayson's plane. Logically, she knew that skydiving accidents were rare. *You're more likely to be killed by a bee sting than skydiving.* She remembered that comment from her own instructor.

But she also remembered the violent jerk and loud pop as her parachute had attempted to deploy. Then spinning, round and round, over and over, and knowing that the all the blood rushing to her feet was not how it was supposed to go.

"Grayson's jumping," his grandfather said. "Will you look at that?"

She did look, barely, mostly unable to breathe through the first few seconds of Grayson's free fall. Then his parachute opened in a perfect canopy and he floated easily to the ground.

By the time she barreled toward him, he had unhooked his shoot and was smiling like a kid who'd had his first successful ride without training wheels—until she plowed her hands into his chest and knocked him on his ass.

"Did you see that?" he asked from the ground, with a big, goofy grin. "It was so amazing. I could see for miles and miles. It was like flying, only more exhilarating."

"What on earth are you trying to prove? You know what? Never mind. I don't care."

Grayson shot to his feet and caught her around the waist. "Jessie wait. Don't you get it? I'm taking a chance I wouldn't normally take. I'm trying to live. Not like I normally do, but like you do."

He turned her around. "I don't know what you did to me in that room in Vegas, but I can't stop thinking about it. I can't stop thinking about you. I'm not selling the romance line. You were right—part of it was for spite. The rest of the decision was ignorance."

She felt her chin tremble. "And you thought jumping out of an airplane would accomplish what?"

He was quiet for a long moment. "I wanted to be more than I normally am. I wanted to feel alive, like you make me feel." He shrugged, looked up at the plane still circling in the air and then back at her. "I came home from that conference after spending a couple of days with you and realized that I work, but I don't do much living."

He tugged on her hips and pulled her close.

She put her hands on his chest to push him back, but didn't quite manage it when he tightened his grip.

"The thought of living my whole life and never again feeling what I felt while making love to you scares the shit out of me." He whispered the words against her ear. "I tried like hell to move on, you know? I buried myself in work, tried to break the Guinness Book of World Records for beer drinking. Nothing helped."

She swiped at the tears rolling down her cheeks. "And when the newness wears off, and you get bored with me?"

"You're the one who told me there are no guarantees, but I think I could search the whole world over and never find anyone less boring than you."

She smiled. "That's probably true."

He brushed his lips over hers. "I'm keeping the romance division. And I'd really like to keep you, for as long as you'll have me."

Losing herself in Grayson felt like the most natural thing in the world, but he'd been honest in Vegas. Quite simply, he was a workaholic. How much could someone really change in a week? "Are you sure you have time for a girlfriend? Especially one who lives in a different state?"

"Well, here's the thing about that. My place is pretty big. I was thinking about getting a roommate. I hear authors make good roommates. You don't happen to know any writers who'd be willing to relocate to New York and shack up with me, do you? I might have a spare bedroom they could use. As an office, not a bedroom."

"You're not serious?"

"I couldn't be more serious. And, those personal assistants you were talking about? Turns out they really do exist. I'm interviewing people for that position next week."

Stunned, she backed up and looked at him. "Who are you, and what have you done with Grayson?"

He took her hands. "I'm falling in love with you, Jess. I think you were right. When you find that one person you care enough about, you make the changes you need to make. I can't promise you that I know exactly how to do this. But I can promise when I screw up, I'll try to make it up to you."

She put her arms around his neck and thoroughly kissed him. He was trying—really trying—to take a chance. "I love you too, Grayson."

"So you'll try it? Moving to New York and staying with me?"

"You know the outlaw. I never walk away from a good challenge."

He put his arms around her and squeezed tight enough

that her feet left the ground. "Come on. Let's get you back home and pack up some stuff. He took her hand and started walking back to the hanger. "By the way. I read your books."

She stopped in her tracks. It was hard to tell how a guy would feel about having his sex life exposed in a novel. "Are you mad?"

His brows drew together. "You mean because you wrote down, verbatim, the sexiest night of my life and put it in a novel that a million people have read—including my grandma and grandpa?"

She winced and waited for him to let her have it. Instead he said, "Not mad so much as curious. If I inspired that Ian sex scene, who inspired the sex scene with the swing and the whip in the other book?"

She smiled and winked. "An outlaw never tells."

Acknowledgments

Thank you to my little "Cosmos with a Twist" family. Tammy Day, Claudia Shelton, and Linda Gilman, you are wonderful critique partners and even better friends. Thank you Dana Waganer for dropping everything and doing a read through with no notice. You rock. And a big thanks to my editor, Lisa Bone, and the whole Entangled team.

Most of all—to my wonderful husband, kids, and mother. Thank you for all you do and being patient while I lock myself away to write. You are the best, and I love you more than words can say.

Michelle

About the Author

Michelle Sharp is a romance author from the Midwest. Although she has a degree in journalism from Southern Illinois University, she finds weaving tales of danger, deception, and love much preferable to reporting the cold, hard facts. Her goal in life? To team resilient, kick-ass heroines with the sexy alpha's who love them. As most writers probably are, she is an avid reader. Her first choice is usually a story with a thrilling combination of danger and love, but any book with a great voice and intriguing story will keep her turning pages well past any reasonable bed-time.